Dance or Get Off the Floor

Copyright 2016

Tina Jones Williams

Bibliographical Data:

Williams, Tina Jones

ISBN: 978-1523701513

General Fiction

Prologue

Over the years, all of the Jamesons have had goals, dreams, and plans; some have been realized spectacularly and others have been kept at bay by circumstances as unexpected as a bolt out of the blue.

Sara and Ben Jameson, along with their four children, are Berkeley transplants from the Southside of Chicago. They are first time home owners in a predominantly Black working-class neighborhood. They have sown the seeds of friendship and grown strong roots in California with three wars, social unrest and vast opportunity as a backdrop.

Over the years, the Jamesons have flourished in their home on Julia Street. Ben and Sara maintained jobs, built enduring relationships, watched and encouraged as the four Jameson siblings grew up, got married, and had children of their own.

Despite the tumultuous times, the Jamesons all managed to make it through the '40s and '50s, mostly unscathed. But life in the '60s was particularly imperfect; particularly 1963, 1965, and 1968 when the country's great leaders were taken in the blink of an eye.

After being lulled into a false sense of hope, Julia Street, the Black community and the nation were reeling from the unspeakable horror of their dreams being killed right before their eyes. Just when it seemed the Fates had taken a holiday they took a more personal tack, deciding the course of events forever.

Life is kind, nearly idyllic

"Hi Mrs. Jameson," called Taunya, Sara's sixteen- year- old next door neighbor. Bubbly and full of life, like Sara's children at that age, Taunya is just what Sara needs in a neighbor. Taunya is light and easy, the embodiment of Sara's feelings. Sara's children, now adults with children of their own have moved away from home and Taunya helps fill the void.

Sara waves hello from her usual spot on the sofa under the front window in the living room of her long-time home on Julia Street. Just a minute later Taunya is at Sara's door carrying a box. Sara knows what this means; Taunya is selling something or more accurately, wants Sara to sell something on her behalf. Sara doesn't mind helping, it requires no effort and causes her no trouble at all. Sara's sales technique is always the same; she simply leaves the box of whatever she's *selling* just inside the front door, next to her most comfortable chair, with an envelope inside for the cash donations. Over time Sara has successfully *sold* popcorn, peanut brittle, and chocolate bars in support of Taunya's cause du jour.

Seeing Taunya at the open door, Sara preempts her knock, calling "Come on in Taunya. What's in the box?"

Full of enthusiasm and energy, Taunya bounces into the living room asking, "Will you help us Mrs. Jameson, we're trying to raise money to charter a bus to go to the Pleasanton County Fair. We're selling tickets for the bus ride and peanut brittle, hopefully we'll make enough money to have refreshments at our next dance at the downtown YMCA," Taunya shared without taking a breath.

Sara is an easy mark for the neighborhood kids. Her house is a hub of activity with people coming and going all the time. She has no shortage of customers buying whatever the girls are selling.

"Sure, is the price clearly marked on the boxes? When is the money due?" asked Sara, confirming her willingness to help.

"Yes, the price is right here," replied Taunya pointing to the top right hand corner of a box she removed from the bigger carton. "We need to turn in our deposit to the bus company in three weeks so I'll check with you then, Mrs. Jameson," replied Taunya in a business-like manner. Thanking Sara for her help, Taunya is gone as quickly as she came.

As she passes the front window, Sara takes note of Taunya's huge afro and her mini-est of miniskirts, both causing Sara to smile. Sara mused that over the twenty-five plus years of looking out of her front window she has been privy to not just the changes in the neighborhood, but in the world.

Although those with whom she had established the closest friendships have moved away, she has become friendly with their replacements. With the changes in the demographic within the neighborhood, Sara acknowledges her role on Julia Street has shifted over the years. As one of the few longtime homeowners left on the block, she is the historian and folklorist, the keeper of the implied rules, social customs and norms, in charge of sharing what *just isn't done*. Her purview is people, music, past and current events and fashion.

Thinking of Taunya's hairstyle and skirt length, Sara realizes she has seen hairstyles and fashion trends come and go with styles becoming more unique to the wearer, not the uniform look of years past. Over time, Sara has seen skirt lengths rise, then fall, silhouettes change from form fitting to nearly shapeless, and back again.

While reminiscing she is reminded of the changes in fashion immediately after World War II. At that time, there was a resurgence of haute couture which trickled down into day and evening wear often seen in the neighborhood. The post-war fashions were very different than the severity of the clothing worn during the War years. Innovations in the textile industry resulted in new fabrications which mimicked expensive luxurious fabrics, but made them more accessible and affordable. Post-war clothing was more beautiful to the eye and to the touch. Sara recalled the women in the community quickly rejected the austerity of wartime fashions, they and their clothing became more elegant and their accessories more ornate. Their wardrobes included perfectly tailored suits, dresses and winter coats made of fine fabrics with buttons that danced and sparkled when they caught the light. Not to be outdone, the men were in their beautifully fitted suits, crisp white shirts, high luster cuff links and tie clips, topped with a perfectly coordinated hat. Unlike in later years, there had been a strict protocol on dressing appropriately for every occasion which was eagerly embraced.

But that was then, and by all accounts current fashion trends are dictated by the young with the norm being skirts for girls and women, the shorter the better, and blue jeans and t-shirts for boys and men. There is a carefree, everybody-doing-their-own-thing attitude that has seeped into every aspect of society. At this point, even Sara feels carefree, life is at that sweet spot where her children are adults, her grandchildren are not yet teens, she is closing in on retirement, and she has fallen in with a bad (meaning good) crowd at UC Berkeley.

Nearly idyllic

*Every silver lining
has a cloud*

The day is picture perfect. The weather conspires spectacularly to make for a memorable occasion. As if to confirm what she already knows Sara checks the newspaper to make sure the scientific prediction matches hers. It does. It would be a gorgeous day.

Sara gets going slowly, taking her time getting dressed, which is in sharp contrast to her habit of being bathed and fully dressed in just over ten minutes. That habit had been rooted in need, with six people and only one bathroom, the art of being a quick change artist was a necessity. But today, with everybody grown up and out, that skill is no longer needed.

Once dressed for the day, Sara makes her way into the kitchen to start a pot of coffee. Just as she settles on the sofa with her mug in hand, the telephone rings. As is her custom, never a fan of the telephone, she prays for grace to handle whatever news is heading her way. Relieved, she listens as her daughter Patrice recounts the plans for the day, wrapping up the conversation with, "Thanks for the call, Patrice. I'll just relax until you all get here." Smiling as she replaces the telephone receiver, Sara reconfirms her belief that God always smiles on her and today is no exception. But, unlike today, she has not always been so pleased with her circumstances. Over the years, Sara has had her share of difficulty, but on this day, Sara is well pleased.

Just as she is taking a sip of coffee, like almost every day at this time, she hears them before she sees them as they make their way to Taunya's house. They are the regulars, announcing their arrival in the way teenagers always do, loud and clear.

"Hey Taunya, you better be up. Last time we had to get your butt out of bed."

Sara chooses to just keep reading her newspaper.

At first, Sara regretted the advice she had given that resulted in Taunya leaving the front door half-open when her guests arrive each morning before school and on the weekend, if her mother had to work. On one such morning, Sara had shared with Taunya, mostly tongue in cheek that it wasn't seemly for young ladies to entertain young men when there were no adults at home to supervise. Rather than curtail the early morning visits Taunya had taken to leaving the front door open so their activities were visible, and hearable, by the entire neighborhood.

Taunya and most of her friends are sophomores and juniors at Berkeley High School, the only public high school in the city. Berkeley High is the melting pot that is Berkeley. Well-off UC Berkeley professors send their children to BHS, children of families living under the poverty line and children of middle class families attend Berkeley High. All ethnicities are represented as well.

Some of Taunya's friends are cheerleaders, some pep squad or song girls, some are members of the

12

marching band, while some of the boys play sports and all are members of the social club they created. It seems to Sara the only purpose of their social club is to socialize. They regularly go on local bus trips, hold dances, have meetings to plan their trips and dances, and get together (often) to practice the dance moves they do while socializing at the dances. Sara knows all of this because most of these activities take place at Tauynya's house right next door.

Sara, though closer to fifty than fifteen, feels almost like a member of the club, mostly because of her proximity to all the action and the support she gives to their activities. In addition to being the "chaperone" next door, regularly helping with fundraisers, when needed, Sara asks her daughter, Patrice, to chaperone their club dances. Patrice, and her lifelong Julia Street friend Nora, always gladly agree. The Julia Street connection is strong.

Today the song blasting from next door is "I Heard it Through the Grapevine," sung loudly by Marvin Gaye. The dance they're practicing is the Hustle. Sara knows this because, in addition to the loud music and finger popping, every so often somebody shouts "Do the Hustle." Instead of being annoyed, Sara is delighted by her neighbor and her friends.

Ignoring the action next door, taking another sip of coffee and reaching for her Winstons, Sara takes stock. Today is a big day for her, the culmination of a closely held goal, and the first step toward the realization of a dream. Today Sara's dreams are within reach, but she is quick to acknowledge that had not always been the case, especially in the recent past. Most of the last decade had

13

been difficult for Sara, for Black people and for the country.

♦

"We are confronted primarily with a moral issue. It is as old as the scriptures and is as clear as the American Constitution." These were the words of hope spoken by President Kennedy in his Civil Rights Address delivered from the Oval Office. This Address was broadcast on the radio and television, which seemed to add weight to the message. Everyone was listening or watching, and in some homes they did both. It seemed that no sooner than those hope-filled words were spoken, the man and his dreams were killed. And in rapid succession other great leaders were eliminated along with their powerful visions for America.

Like dominos they fell, one after another over a five-year span, taking hope with them; Medgar Evers, President Kennedy, Malcolm X, Dr. Martin Luther King Jr. and just months later Robert Kennedy. It felt like a punch to the gut each time, but the assassination of Robert Kennedy felt more personal. During his campaign for President, while riding a Southern Pacific boxcar, the train stopped on Sacramento Street, just steps from Sara's home. Sara had joined the crowd that had assembled to see him on his way to the UC Berkeley campus. Even now Sara is not able to shake the despair she felt when each of these great men had been murdered.

Before Sara can go too far down this sad path she hears her name being called from outside. It is Zachary, Taunya's eight-year-old brother. He and Sara have been friends since he was a tiny boy when he brought her flowers from his garden, sometime with the snails still attached.

"Sara, can I come in?" he called from the driveway. "The music is too loud at my house. They keep playing the same song over and over, singing loud and dancing!"

"You can come in Zachary, but I don't have much time today; remember I have plans," replied Sara. She smiles as she thinks of the sight of Zachary running back from the cleaners with her graduation gown flying behind him after picking it up as a favor for her.

"That's okay. My mom's not home and I'm supposed to stay with Taunya, but I can't hear the TV 'cause they're dancing and singing again. Oh man, I can hear them over here, too. Can I use your telephone, I'm gonna call my mom's work," Zachary complained.

Calming him down with an offer of peanut brittle (from the box she is *selling*) and with his choice of television show, the crisis is averted. When the music stops, Zachary returns home, allowing Sara to take care of a few finishing touches.

♦

"Mama, we're here," calls Ronald as he comes into the house.

"I'll be right out," says Sara dabbing a bit of her favorite perfume, My Sin, behind her ears and on her wrists.

Before she sees anyone else she sees her mother.

"What a beautiful day for a graduation," says her mother, Tessa Crawford. She had come from Los Angeles for the graduation and a short visit.

Seeing her mother, Sara is suddenly overcome by the enormity of the occasion.

She couldn't help thinking of her last graduation day, over thirty years ago, when she had been rewarded a full scholarship to her first choice college for her straight 'A' high school performance. Circumstances had gotten in the way, and due to the lack of money, there wasn't even enough to cover incidentals, so Sara had not been able to attend.

But that had all changed when, as an almost fifty-year old woman, Sara had been accepted into the University of California at Berkeley, today would be graduating from the University, and with stellar grades. Another reason to smile, Sara has been accepted into Graduate School to pursue a Masters Degree in Folklore. She is overcome by the enormity of the day.

"Mama." One word said it all as they fell into an embrace. To Sara, her mother is the most selfless, kind, wise, gentle, compassionate, talented woman she has ever known. Theirs is a mutual admiration club, a pleasure to behold.

On this day Sara couldn't help thinking of her father, saddened his health had stopped him from being a part of the occasion. Not knowing how her father and mother would feel about being together again, Sara thought things had turned out best. Sara's father had called the other night to congratulate her and tell her how proud he is of her. As usual, theirs was a long, rambling conversation that took them to a place they had not been before—a discussion of Sara's relatives on his side of the family. Due to circumstances which Sara had never fully understood, she had not met many of them and he spoke very little of those she had not met. Fear of adding to the obvious sadness he felt about his family kept Sara from pushing the topic. Following his lead, over the years her father tended to sprinkle facts about the family as if they were bread crumbs along the way.

That night he started by sharing that her grandfather had been White of German descent, married to a very fair complexioned Colored woman, this much Sara already knew. He went on to describe their children, he and his siblings, as "light, bright, and damned near White." Two of the children, his brother and sister, who would have been Sara's uncle and aunt, were able to pass for White—and they did. This *was* new to Sara.

He explained it had been 1915, segregation was at its height and his brother and sister were encouraged to take the opportunity fate had handed them. It was a sad reality for the family. Once they walked through that door *to the other side*, for their own safety and the safety of the rest of the family, they could never come back. And they could never chance having children for fear the "Colored" genes would be evident in the children.

Sara felt that even if it was best for her *lost* uncle and aunt, her family tree had been altered forever in ways she would never even know.

Every silver lining has a cloud

♦

They were all there, Sara's and Ben's children, Tessa (of course named for Sara's mother), Ronald, Gregory, Patrice, the grandchildren, and Ben. Though living apart, Sara's relationship with Ben is complicated. All those years ago, when they met just a few blocks away from DuSable High School in a little record shop on the Southside of Chicago, he courted and married her. He is the father of her children, he provided them a home, moved the family to Berkeley where they found broader opportunities, changing their lives forever. It is impossible for Sara to consider her life without considering Ben.

♦

Taking in the sights as they rode down Sacramento Street, Sara silently agreed with her mother, it is indeed a beautiful day for a graduation. As UC campus came into view, Carl exclaimed, "There's your school Grandma."

"Yes, it is Carl. I had no idea I would be so excited to see it today. I almost said aloud, 'There's my school Carl.'" That is one of the inside jokes they share.

The campus and surrounding area is jam-packed with people, some dressed to the nines and others in blue jeans and earth shoes, the dichotomy that is Berkeley. The grounds at UC Berkeley are meticulous and the sun is shining as bright as the planned futures of the graduates. It is a beautiful day for a graduation.

"I will drop you off here, Sara, so you can join the others," said Ben as he slowed to a stop in a turn-around filled with graduates in their regalia.

Sara grabbed her cap and gown off of the hook on the passenger side of the backseat, and said "see you later" before joining a group of fellow grads.

"Look at Grandma," said Carl with his usual enthusiasm. "She's putting on her hat and coat like the other people. Are we going to see her inside?" he asked somewhat anxiously.

"Yes. After we park the car we will walk back over here and find our seats for the graduation ceremony. We'll be back in plenty of time to see them as they walk in all dressed in their caps and gowns. They will walk in alphabetically by last name, so look for your grandma in the crowd. Grandma's last name is Jameson so what letters come before and after ' j'?" asked Ben.

"A-b-c-d-e-f-g-h-i-j-k-, i comes before j and k comes after it," replied Carl with confidence.

"We'll watch as all of the students come in but we will really pay attention when the ones with last names starting with 'I' come in so we will be ready to take pictures as your grandma walks by," instructed Ben with a smile. Ben was grateful that Carl didn't ask how they would know what the graduates' last names were because he didn't have an answer.

Sara's mother had been silently taking in the day, filled with pride and love for her daughter, her only child. Never once has she doubted Sara's abilities, or that she would end up in this place on this day. One of her favorite scriptures is "When the Lord delights in a man's path He makes his steps firm." Sara's steps have been firm since the day she accepted the offer of admission to UC Berkeley, and today is further affirmation.

Finding their seats was a bit of an adventure as there were some in attendance who had started "celebrating" before the ceremony, but no harm done, everyone was in a festive mood. Team Jameson was able to find an entire row, placing the grandkids in the middle bound by adults at both ends.

"There she is, there she is, take a picture!" shouted the grandkids, with Ronald complying by taking several shots as Sara made her way to her seat. The speeches were inspirational and brief (which the grandkids appreciated as much as most of the graduates), but Sara was taken with the messages, relishing the experience. She especially liked the descriptions of the ways in which the graduates would change the world by starting their own company, writing the next best seller, while knowing she would have the earth changing task of doing the laundry the next day. The contrast made her smile.

Changing her tassel from right to left as her degree was conferred, Sara felt an excitement that was shared with the family, but the sense of accomplishment was hers alone.

♦

Tessa Crawford's short stay was to be filled to the brim with family and friends. Friday, the day of her arrival, she, along with the rest of the family witnessed family history first hand. Not only had Sara attended a prestigious university, but had graduated with high honors. As if to make the dream complete, after the ceremony, Sara introduced her mother to several of her professors, making the introductions with obvious love and pride.

It was a beautiful graduation.

On the ride home, the grandkids took turns wearing Sara's cap and once they got home, each took a turn in full regalia.

"Look at me, Grandma," shouted Rose, Ronald's daughter. "I have on your hat and coat."

"It's called a cap and gown," corrected Sara gently.

"I'm gonna wear a cap and gown when I graduate college," said Rose with confidence.

"From your lips to God's ear," murmured Sara.

Guests, including several of Sara's professors, arrived just in time to hear James Brown sing "Say It Loud I'm Black and I'm Proud," signaling the start of the party. For the rest of the evening most everybody danced and sang along until later, when the children took themselves to bed and the after party started.

Although Sara and her outstanding accomplishments were the reason for the party, the party itself was just like all the rest hosted on Julia Street, dancing, drinking and eating until the wee hours. The fact that three of Sara's professors were in the house didn't change the tone and tenor of the celebration. Nobody seemed to mind hearing "I'm Black and I'm Proud," for four hours–understanding that it must be Sara's Song.

♦

The house was quiet the next morning after a wonderful celebration. Both Sara and her mother had taken advantage of the quiet and slept in. After a light breakfast, enjoying the opportunity to be together Tessa stood and stretched.

"I'm going to visit Bell for a while," shared Mrs. Crawford as she headed into the kitchen to replace her coffee cup.

Bell is one of Tessa Crawford's oldest and dearest friends, living right around the corner on California and Ashby. She and Tessa became friends when Tessa was living with Sara and Ben when the children were very young. Tessa often fondly recalled Bell's kindness to the children as they passed her home every morning as she walked them to Lincoln Elementary School, Ronald being in kindergarten and Tessa in first grade. The children had appreciated her kindness as well. In those days, Tessa had often heard them remark, "Miss Bell's voice sounds just like a bell." When they didn't think Tessa was listening, because of Bell's short round physique, one might say "Miss Bell is sort of the same shape as a bell." But not once did they say it in a mean way.

"I'm sure she'll be delighted to see you," replied Sara from her spot on the sofa as Tessa crossed the threshold. Sara then planned an afternoon of reflection, glad for the solitude.

Hours later when Mrs. Crawford returned, by her account, the visit had been a success with the two old friends reminiscing and making plans to attend church the next morning. They planned to attend their home church, Ephesians Church of God in Christ on the corner of King and Alcatraz, just a few blocks from Bell's home. The church had been in that location since 1936 and the women had joined in 1944. They had attended faithfully while Tessa was living in Berkeley and whenever she came back for a visit. Bell attended weekly.

After a fulfilling church service, and a quick return trip to her bookie to pick up her winnings, it was time for Mrs. Crawford to go to the airport to go back home. Parting was much easier now that PSA had flights to Los Angeles for thirty-nine dollars roundtrip, leaving every hour on the hour. Even though the visit had been lovely, and they had definite plans to see each other again, soon, the miles between them sometimes seemed insurmountable.

Every silver lining has a cloud

She isn't the ringleader . . .
this time

Sara takes her role as family and neighborhood folklorist seriously, feeling it is her responsibility to gather and share information that might otherwise be lost. She is particularly fluent in all things Black and Berkeley. Today she is taking a look back at just a few years earlier when people in general had been both disillusioned and angry, with the students at Berkeley High and UC Berkeley no exception, particularly the Black student body. At that time the country had been shrouded in a shared sadness. Regardless of personal philosophy, *your* chosen leader had just been cut down in his prime. Whether you believed in a non-violent approach, using the political process to solve inequities, or aggressively taking what you thought was well deserved, *your* leader had been cut down in his prime.

Not knowing exactly what to do, Black and sympathetic White students in Berkeley were demanding change at the high school and university level. In response to student concerns, in1969, the Black History Department, the only one of its kind in the United States, was created to provide a unique learning environment within Berkeley High School.

At about the same time, a small group of esteemed professors got together and made a pitch to the

Administration to add Black History to the UC Berkeley curriculum. That is what educators do: whenever there is a problem they suggest "educating" your way out of it. Timing and good fortune being everything, among the very talented professors were Sarah with an h, Adrienne with two e's and two n's, and Barbara, just Barbara, who together were a triple threat. Any one of them alone is talented, accomplished and noteworthy but the three of them together create the perfect storm – in a good way. The climate had been right for change and the group of professors was certain if they built it, they would come. They were right. The Black Studies Department at University of California at Berkeley became a fully accepted reality under their leadership in the late 1960s.

Years later, Black Studies (now called African American Studies) at UC Berkeley and Berkeley High continues to be much more than just an academic department. The programs have provided connections to the local community. They have brought the surrounding community to campus, bringing the campus to the surrounding community.

♦

When Sara was completing her undergrad degree, the Black Studies department had only been up and running for a few months with just thirty class offerings in the course catalog. Fortunately, she had the opportunity to take classes from and become friendly with Sarah, Adrienne and Barbara, who taught undergrad courses in addition to graduate coursework. Based on Sara's work they had individually and collectively encouraged Sara to pursue her Master's Degree in Folklore. They believe, and Sara was inclined to agree, that she is a talented storyteller.

Sara sailed through her first year in the masters program, melding her love of music with her love of words, the timing and the mix couldn't have been better. Continuing to do her job on the swing shift at the Oakland Army Base, knowing that in twelve years she will have enough time in service to retire with full benefits at age 62.

Still the late night and weekend place to be, the guests at Sara's home are eclectic and multi-ethnic and multi-generational. It is not uncommon for Sara to entertain her children and their friends, their children, students and professors from school, her friends from work, as well as neighbors, all at the same time. The best part of Sara's life, of course, is her family. Her adult children, with young children of their own, live within walking distance of Sara and visit often.

♦

The neighborhood has continued to change, allowing Sara to long for the old days while embracing the new. The neighbors to Sara's right are fairly new to Julia Street. They are a couple about her age with a son not as old as her children but several years older than the high school kids in the neighborhood. The couple are friendly enough, but they keep to themselves. Their son seems to be struggling to find his way. Sara heard through the neighborhood grapevine that he had joined the army and is waiting to be sent to Viet Nam. Sara prays the grapevine is wrong.

On Sara's left are Taunya, her little brother Zachary and their mother, Vivian. Sara has never heard Vivian speak of her husband, the children's father, and Sara has never brought him up. The little threesome seems to function well together as a unit and they are kind and inclusive to others in the neighborhood. Much of Taunya's life seems to play out in front of Sara, either next door with the door open or right in front of her living room window. And what didn't play out, she heard about; the frat games, step shows, trips to Oakland and Richmond, and the twice weekly house parties with friends nearly every Friday and Saturday night. Not to mention what seems like endless shopping for all of their activities. All that is needed to shop without a parent in tow is a parent's credit card or a signed blank check (with the name of the store and amount filled in at the time of purchase) and a note saying you have your parent's approval to shop using their credit card or check.

Sara has never seen or heard anything she felt the need to share with Taunya's mother, although she would not hesitate to do so, if the need arose. Sara is quite sure Taunya's mother would welcome feedback from an interested bystander. Sara thought Vivian, unlike others in the neighborhood, would welcome a second pair of eyes because at this point, husbands are in short supply on the 1500 block of Julia Street. Single mothers are parenting singularly.

♦

"T-T-T-O-C", "T-T-T-O-C." Today is not the first time Sara has heard this chant outside her window. The last time was at the same time last year, but before that, it was when her children were in high school. A big year for TOC frenzy was in 1963 when Patrice was a senior at Berkeley High.

The TOC – Tournament of Champions was a Bay Area High School Basketball Tournament which got its start in 1947. The Tournament of Champions was a postseason basketball competition that determined the Northern California champion each year from 1947 through 1975. The tournament was sponsored by three Bay Area high school leagues.

Followers of basketball feel there was nothing like the TOC for overall strength of competition and popularity. During its lifetime, the tournament attracted more than 475,000 hoops fans to several Bay Area venues. In its first four seasons, the tournament was held at several venues in the Bay Area from Cal Berkeley to Kezar Pavilion in San Francisco, back to Cal and then to the City College of San Francisco gym. The Tournament was later held in Berkeley from 1951 until 1967 when it moved into the new and larger Oakland Coliseum Arena, where it was held until the final game in 1975.

A keepsake Tournament program was published every year starting in 1948. The first edition filled eight pages, with participant rosters, and sold for a dime. By 1953, team photos had been added on glossy paper which included a rundown of previous tournament results and records. The price jumped to a quarter in 1958 and the program was expanded to 20 pages, which included individual photos of star players and a section with pictures of game action, rooting sections and cheer stunts, school mascots and cheerleaders, plus the awards ceremonies. By 1975, which was the last year of the Tournament of Champions, the format had been vastly improved and the price was 75 cents, definitely a collector's item. A total of 318 games were played by teams from 82 schools since the tournament's inception.

During the 1960s, schools often in the hunt for inclusion in the tournament games were Berkeley, Richmond, Harry Ells and McClymonds. McClymonds further distinguished itself by ending their run with six consecutive TOC wins to its credit, including the 1963 championship. In the narrowest victory in a TOC championship game, McClymonds captured its sixth consecutive crown with a 66-65 overtime win over Berkeley, a heartbreaker for Yellow Jacket fans. During that game, there were seven ties and 11 lead changes. The game remained close throughout and wound up setting a new single game combined scoring record of 131 points.

The 1970 Championship (the games Taunya and friends were so looking forward to) was won by Berkeley High, home of the Yellow Jackets, 70-64. Berkeley's Big Three led the way as Glen Burke scored 22, Marvin Buckley 20, and John Lambert 18. The BHS Cheerleaders also earned a place in TOC history by winning a spirit award during the 1970 games.

Moving to her open front door, seeing Taunya passing by, Sara called, "Taunya, here is the money for the peanut brittle I've sold."

"Oh wow, thanks Mrs. Jameson. The pep squad is having uniforms made for the TOC rally by a lady who lives down by Longfellow. This money is just in time. I really appreciate it," said Taunya accepting the cash.

"With all the activity going on I couldn't help but know that Berkeley High is going to the TOC again, exciting times," said Sara. "By the way, let me know if the peanut brittle money isn't right. I know I've shared a couple boxes with Zachary and I may not have put the money in the envelope."

"Will do, thanks for everything. I've been meaning to tell you, thank you for being nice to Zachary, he loves coming to your house, there is always something going on," said Taunya.

You're a fine one to talk thought Sara with a smile, thinking of the almost constant happenings next door.

"Well, I enjoy his company as well, and he seems to have developed a real love for music and an ear for Jazz. Sometimes I quiz him asking, 'Who's that on sax,' or 'who's that singing,' and he's almost always right. I enjoy sharing my music with him," smiled Sara.

"Well, he loves it. Gotta go, there's a club meeting tonight and you'll be glad to know it's at somebody else's house.

No noise from me and my friends tonight. Thanks again Mrs. Jameson," said Taunya, returning Sara's smile as she headed down the stairs.

She isn't the ringleader . . . this time

*Maybe she should have
seen it coming*

In 1943, when the Jameson family moved into their brand new home on Julia Street, the neighborhood was mostly working-class Colored families made up of two working parents and at least a couple of kids. Almost every home was owned by the occupant and Sacramento Street boasted an array of Colored-owned businesses. If needed, Sara could bundle up a sick child and take him right across the street to Dr. Anderson's office. If a prescription was written, it could be filled a few doors down at Rumford's Pharmacy. Clothes could be cleaned, shoes repaired, hair done, notions, and jewelry bought at businesses owned by Colored people. In those days, Sara liked to say, "Everything we need is right here, we never have to leave the neighborhood."

After 1969, things in the neighborhood were the same, but different. There were still a few of the original businesses on Sacramento Street– Greer's Jewelry, Sacramento Market (owned by a Chinese family), and both liquor stores. But Sara rarely frequented these shops; she did her grocery shopping at Co-op on Ashby and Telegraph and bought her costume jewelry at Capwells in El Cerrito Plaza.

Unchanged from the early days, there is still a group of men standing in front of the small liquor store on

Sacramento Street, but the faces have changed and so have their choices. Most of the new group are younger than the men they had replaced, younger than Sara's children but older than Taunya and her friends. These new men had been out of school (either dropped out or graduated), long enough to "have a life plan." But no such luck, it seems their *plan* is to have more to drink or to score more drugs. Their activities are visible and unsettling to the Julia Street residents. Where, in the past, there had been a periodic police presence in the neighborhood, now a police bus parked on the corners of Sacramento and Julia around the clock.

Maybe she should have seen it coming.

Sara and her friend, Mary, Sara's first friend on Julia Street, spent hours lamenting the changes that had taken place in the neighborhood over the years. Chief among them is the shift in the makeup of the families and the fact, when long term residents moved away apartment buildings were replacing single family homes, changing the neighborhood demographics dramatically. To them, it seems the new families, mostly single mothers with young children, have a different set of challenges than those faced by Sara and Mary when they were starting out. They conceded that with both parents in the home, and the help of their mothers they did not face the same battles the new families would have ahead of them.

♦

To Sara, looking at the new group standing on Sacramento Street, it feels like something is broken, as if the bridge from adolescence to adulthood has been burned resulting in a group of particularly ill-prepared, ill-equipped young Black men. Sara couldn't help but wonder what had gone wrong during the years since her youngest child, Patrice, had graduated from high school in 1963.

Talking it over with family and friends, the theories were as varied as those offering them. Most were careful not to trivialize or suggest the root causes were simplistic.

Some blame the "breakdown in the family," with so many Black boys being parented by just their mothers, with fathers not in the picture. Mothers struggle to meet basic needs becoming overwhelmed, those feelings spilling over onto her son.

Others believe these young men are navigating in a world that is hostile, starting as early as elementary school. There is a belief that, to teachers, certain behaviors exhibited by Black boys are cause for concern but ignored in their White peers. Often *at wits end* teachers send Black boys out of the classroom as a form of discipline. The result, the child falls behind, which can be tied to behavior issues– a vicious cycle. All of this is feeding into the notion that the world is hostile, with Black boys, and ultimately Black men being generally under suspicion.

Still others offer the flagging economy as the culprit, citing the higher numbers of unemployed Black men as compared to their White peers.

Some, mostly men, suggest it's "their own damn fault."

They all could agree the Viet Nam War devastated men between the ages of eighteen to twenty five, particularly poor Black men. These men were particularly impacted, unlike their wealthier White peers who were able to avoid the draft, if they chose, by enrolling in college or in more extreme cases by moving to Canada. Having neither of those options, many young Black men either served their country in a war they neither supported nor understood, or disappeared in plain sight, never holding a "real" job, owning property, or being a fully functioning contributor to society. Many of the young men who went to Viet Nam came back different than when they left, a shell of themselves, physically or mentally disabled, many attempting to self medicate using drugs and or alcohol. All of these scenarios contributing to the already overwhelmingly complex question of "Where do young Black men fit in the larger society?"

♦

She felt it before she saw it. At first she chalked it up to the general malaise she felt after watching the nightly news. There were regular updates on the war, the number of casualties on both sides and the protesters, images from both sides. But the most chilling were the visuals and interviews of the soldiers returning to the states.

"Saigon roads were dirt, homes were tar paper and aluminum shacks, and there were pigs and chickens in every yard."

"Those were the first men I killed and I remember each of them very distinctly."

"It broke my heart and the heart of the men I served with."

The interviews of the returning soldiers left Sara bereft.

♦

She felt it before she saw it. It seemed to be seeping from under the doors and under the window sills. The house seemed to be shrouded in sadness. Sara hadn't heard anything directly, or through the neighborhood grapevine, so she wasn't on alert. At first, she chose to dismiss it, thought it was coincidence or just bad timing. As the realization was settling in, Sara cursed the placement of her kitchen window, wishing it was anywhere other than directly across from her neighbors' window.

For so long she had known next to nothing about the couple next door, just that they are friendly teachers about her age fairly new to Julia Street, and they have one child, a son who is serving in Viet Nam. Now as a result of their misplaced kitchen windows, Sara knows far more than she ever would want to know. And now that she knows, what should she do with the information?

She tried varying her routine, cooking dinner a little earlier, having her coffee a little later, and drinking water only when necessary. But nothing helped. Most every time Sara went into her kitchen there she was, sitting at her own table just a few feet away in her kitchen, not knowing or not caring that Sara was privy to her private misery. Head down, glass in hand and bottle sitting at the ready, hour after hour, day after day, and night after night. It got worse when her son, her boy, came home from Viet Nam.

Before he left, Sara had feared he was a little lost but upon his return she was certain. Every day, the scene played out just the same, with him sitting on the front porch, smoking one cigarette after another. He would then get up and walk head down, from one end of the block to the other, all day long. Some nights he would still be walking when she got home from work. Some nights, Sara saw his mother gently leading her son, her boy, back home.

The war's tearing families apart.

♦

There are all kinds of sadness and Sara was feeling it from both sides. Tauyna, was graduating from high school and taking an apartment in Oakland with a friend. It would leave a void in the neighborhood, leaving Sara just a little sad.

Sara was attending the graduation and as Taunya had to be there early, was driving Vivian and Zachary to the ceremony.

Class of 1970 Berkeley High School graduation ceremony, like so many classes before, was being held at the Greek Theater which sits proudly on the University of California acreage and is nothing short of spectacular. It was designed in 1903 in the image of an ancient Greek theater, seating 8,500. It is a favorite music venue, hosting Jazz, Pop, Rock artists and their fans.

It was on the drive that Vivian shared what Sara already suspected, that they had no family in the area. Sara suggests they have a meal afterward down on the Berkeley Marina at H's Lordships.

In typical Berkeley style the weather was mild and beautiful. Also in typical Berkeley style the student speeches were just controversial enough. Taunya was lovely in her purple dress covered by her gold gown. The boys wore red, as Berkeley High school colors are red and gold. As Taunya passed by in the processional Zachary shouted, "There she is. Hey, Taunya!" In response she blew him a kiss.

The food at H's Lordships is always reliably good, the conversation was light and everyone enjoyed their table by the window with the spectacular view of the Bay Bridge. As the meal was winding down, Sara sensed the pull Taunya was starting to feel between duty to family and fun with friends. Sara chose to make it easy for her, suggesting she drop Taunya off at a friend's home. Met with a smile of thanks from Taunya, Sara knew she had done the right thing. Vivian invited Sara to join them for coffee and cake back at their house. Zachary opted for ice cream with his cake.

♦

Sara missed Taunya's energy and she even missed Taunya's friends. The singing, dancing, chanting and everything associated with being teenagers was gone. Sara missed the constant parade to Taunya's house, her friends wearing what could be called the uniform of the day; girls in miniskirts and platforms for school or bell bottom jeans and platforms for the weekend, boys dressed in Angel Flight polyester wide bell bottom slacks paired with vivid patterned, wide collared polyester shirts worn unbuttoned, highlighting a peace sign medeallion, and platforms for dress up. Sara missed their entrepreneurial, adventurous spirit, the constant planning, and the amiable rebelling. It was Taunya and her friends who had decided it was too cold for them to wear skirts one winter morning (the coldest on record), so for the first time in the history of Berkeley High, the girls wore pants to school. And they kept wearing them.

Gone was the direct pipeline into all things teenager. Sara felt a sadness that was akin to how she felt when her youngest child left home. It was as though some of the light had left the neighborhood.

Maybe she should have seen it coming

Sara's got a brand new bag

Maybe she had wished to join a tribe, a clan, a club, a rowdy, boisterous fellowship; all for one, one for all. Maybe he had longed for one-on-one, he and she against the world; intimacy, closeness, familiarity, but neither one had informed the other. Ben considered this notion, not for the first time, as he parked his car in the driveway at the house on the 1500 block of Julia Street. The home where he built the second story, relocated the master bedroom and added the large picture window and the small balcony. The home where he no longer lived.

After his customary two taps on the front door, and without waiting for a response, he crossed the threshold to a usually unheard-of silence.

"Sara," he said, spotting her on the sofa surrounded by a stack of books and papers in her lap, "no music again today? This is the third time I've come in and there's no music playing. Why is that?"

Before responding, Sara thought, *how interesting*. Ben had gone on record years ago with his lack of interest in music, saying openly, time and time again in front of all who were present, "I don't care if any of them ever play another note." That simple statement had broken Sara's heart every time he made it.

"Working on this degree in Folklore, I've discovered written words that are lyrical, musical on their own. When I read these words, they have a rhythm, a melody that is reminiscent of my favorite songs. If I read and listen to music at the same time it's like listening to two songs at once. I can't do it," replied Sara.

"That must be a tough choice for you, having to pick one over the other," said Ben, genuinely trying to empathize.

"Most of the time it's not a problem. There are times that call for the written word and other times ask for music. There have been a few times when I have read something that required following up with a specific song. I can't really explain it, I guess you had to be there, or in your case, maybe not," Sara replied with just a shadow of a smile.

Ben made no comment. He would be the first to admit he never really understood Sara's music or her feelings about it, and now here was something new that he didn't quite understand. Ben knew this was no minor misunderstanding, but a major disconnect, and in no small part, it had contributed to the end of their marriage. He knew there were other issues, much bigger issues, some they hadn't even named.

Both had grown weary of the endless arguing about topics that were never the real topic, so they had decided to split. There had been a trigger, not catastrophic unless you call two people who had broken each others' hearts over and over, catastrophic. Sara had loved music, Ben didn't. Sara had enjoyed company, Ben didn't. Ben enjoyed quiet, Sara didn't. Sara had coddled her sons, Ben didn't. Sara was a homebody, Ben wasn't. Add to all that, the lure of Sacramento Street and the women and there was the trigger.

Ben had moved out of the house on Julia Street, but neither had entirely moved on. They had simply released each other from roles that perhaps they should never have been asked to play. They ended their contract but not their relationship.

On the day Ben moved out Sara gave up arguing, vowing never again to raise her voice in anger, choosing to let her words, her tone, inflection and look on her face tell the tale.

Ben was also weary, and by mutual consent they no longer had unmet expectations of each other. It was not lost on either of them that perhaps if things had been different in the early days, perhaps things would be different now.

◆

"We can't keep having this conversation, said Sara in earnest. "We have a job to do and as long as we accept a paycheck from the U.S. Government, that is exactly what we are going to do."

"I just hate this war so much," replied Verniece, one of Sara's most conscientious employees. "It's done irreparable damage to so many people, on both sides."

"I can't disagree," acquiesced Sara.

Sara is a true American. She first worked in support of WWII in 1943 as a welder at the Richmond Shipyards, and now works in support of the Viet Nam war effort in MOTBA, Military Ocean Terminal Bay Area at the Oakland Army Base, known as the gateway into and out of Viet Nam. It is not unusual for Sara to see the soldiers as they are shipped out or upon their arrival stateside. She sees their faces and she knows who she is working for.

Sara's group is charged with getting soldiers and cargo where they are supposed to be, intact and on time, and she has never let her personal feelings about war and its efficacy get in the way of doing her job. On every front Sara is forced to face her feelings. At the University there are regular anti-war demonstrations, sometime resulting in police intervention. At home Sara's children and visitors are vocal about their disdain for the war, not to

46

mention the constant reminder of the affect it had on her neighbors and their son, Terrance. At work her subordinates use her as a sounding board for their feelings on the evils of war. Sometimes it's too much.

♦

Almost every night on her drive home from the Base, Sara reminds herself it's the soldiers she is working for, and asking herself what she can do for the soldier who lives next door. She secretly hopes she won't see him walking his well-worn path when she pulls into her driveway. Most nights Sara's prayers are not answered and as she rounds the corner she can see him, head down, slowly retracing his steps, as if trying to discover where things went so terribly wrong. Often, Sara muses that his father, though living in the home, is strangely absent from these scenes. It's just the two of them, Terrance's mother silently drinking at the kitchen table and her son silently drifting up and down the block before she gently guides him back home. On this night Sara's decides she has to do something.

Sara is a praying woman, taking her issues, concerns, joys and sorrows to God. Unlike her mother, who prays all the time, whispering her thanksgiving throughout the day and night, Sara falls to her knees twice a day, once when she opens her eyes in the morning and again before she closes them at night. Like her mother,

Sara has been a faithful church member since her family moved to Berkeley. They first belonged to Bethlehem Lutheran Church on 12th and Myrtle in Oakland. When her beloved pastor died Sara began attending Bethlehem Lutheran Church on Telegraph in Berkeley, it is closer to home and it doesn't hurt that it's right across the street from the Smokehouse, one of Sara's favorite spots.

Sara takes her commitments as a parishioner seriously; she tithes, supports special funds and places flowers at the altar each Sunday during the birth months of each of her children. Sara knows the importance of active spirituality and believes in the power of prayer. So on this night Sara prays for a meaningful way to intervene on behalf of her neighbors.

As is often the case after a night of specific prayer Sara wakes with an answer and quickly makes a plan. Sara has a change in perspective; she no longer feels helpless, she feels invested.

◆

Sara couldn't get to work fast enough. However, the traffic along Highway 80 was not her friend; the artery leading to Oakland and San Francisco was clogged as usual. Finally arriving at the Base, Sara places her handbag in her desk drawer and hangs her shawl on the peg behind her chair.

"Hey, Sara," call her colleagues as they make their way to their desks. Sara replies with friendly greetings of her own.

"I need to check in with Bob. I'll be back in just a few minutes," said Sara, not signaling the importance of her errand. No one took particular notice as Sara, the shift supervisor often met with employees in other units. Hurrying down the long corridor, Sara rehearsed her plea, hoping not to give too much away for the sake of privacy, but sharing enough to encourage a favorable response.

"Sara, what brings you to our neck of the woods," asked Bob as he walks down the hall in Sara's direction. He is just the man Sara wants to see.

"Bob, I'm glad you're here. Can I have a few minutes of your time, in your office?" asked Sara.

"My time is your time," replied Bob. He knows Sara well enough to know she has a serious matter on her mind.

"Have a seat," said Bob closing the office door.

"Thanks. I'm not going to waste our time with a lot of unnecessary detail. There's a soldier who needs our help," shared Sara.

Within minutes of sharing the story, Sara has a plan, resources and a different perspective.

Sara's got a brand new bag

Two things can be true

"Let me see, let me see!"

"Oh, it's so pretty, when did you get it?"

"What did he say?

"What did you say?"

Sara thought her imagination was getting the better of her, thought it was wishful thinking, but looking out of her window she saw some of the light had come back to the neighborhood. There was Taunya, surrounded by her group of friends, each taking their turn looking at her left hand. Sara had heard from Zachary, of course, that "Taunya is trying to get married." Not sure what that meant, Sara had decided to wait for a more credible and less cryptic source.

Spotting Sara in the window, Taunya yelled above her friends' chatter, "Hi Mrs. Jameson, have you heard?"

"Hi Taunya. Good to see you. Want to come in for a minute?" asked Sara in response.

"Sure," replied Taunya brightly.

Taunya and her friends moved as a unit toward Sara's front porch and through the front door. Sara recognized all of them but was unsure of their names. She chose instead to greet them with, "Hi girls, I hear Taunya has news."

They all squealed as Taunya extended her left hand. "We're getting married in July. My mom thinks we should wait till I'm done with college but we're sure everything will work out," said Taunya, as usual without taking a breath, and with the confidence of youth.

Sara is informed enough to know that 'we' meant Taunya and the boyfriend she'd been dating since they were in high school, who will be graduating from college in June with a degree in engineering. Sara was not surprised to hear Taunya's mother preferred she would wait until she finished college before getting married. Sara knows with absolute certainty that Zachary wishes Taunya would move back home and forget the whole thing.

◆

The wedding was held just a few months later on a sultry mid-July evening at Sara's church on Telegraph Avenue in Berkeley. Because they did not have a church home of their own, Taunya's mother had asked Sara if she would arrange the use of the church for the ceremony and the hall for the reception, and Sara had been happy to do it.

The church by design is austere; the Lutherans eschew the opulence of the Catholic Church from which they seceded. The altar was not overly decorated, just a lush floral display on either side of the pulpit in the colors of the wedding. Because it was summer and the days are longer, the stained glass windows and the subdued light from the sconces that line the walls cast a lovely glow.

Guests arrived to the sounds of a lone pianist playing songs selected by Taunya and her mother. It was obvious to Sara who had chosen each song.

After a short musical interlude the wedding party assembled at the altar. The bridal attendants were lovely in tangerine voile and the groom and groomsmen were handsome in coordinating tuxes. Sara recognized many members of the wedding party from Taunya's days on Julia Street.

At the sound of the wedding march, the sanctuary doors opened and all eyes were on the bride who was very pretty in a white long-sleeved empire dress with lace and pearls inset on the bodice and on the veil. She was escorted by a youngish man Sara had seen visiting next door.

Sara thought the ceremony was beautiful. The musical selections, a blend of soft contemporary pieces and standard wedding fare, and the time of day --six pm-- added to the solemnity of the occasion. The bride and groom seemed in tune with one another, whispering and sharing a private joke before they were pronounced man and wife.

The reception was nicely done in a comfortably accommodating manner. The hall, with its archways and moldings reminiscent of Tudor design, popular in medieval architecture, is a spacious and welcoming space. The floral arrangements moved from the altar, sat on the buffet table providing just the right amount of adornment. The food was tasty and plentiful. No alcohol was served, but the guests who seemed to be enjoying themselves, didn't seem to miss it. After about the third piece of cake, even Zachary seemed to be reconciled to the marriage. Sara stayed for the entire reception, but begged off attending the after party, wishing the newlyweds well.

"Thank you for everything, Mrs. Jameson. Thanks to you, my wedding was everything I hoped for," said Tuanya as Sara was leaving the reception.

"It was entirely my pleasure Taunya. I wish you every happiness." replied Sara warmly as she headed up the stairs to the church exit.

Arriving back home, Sara was pleased to see her "walking" neighbor, Terrance, was nowhere to be seen which, she hoped, spoke well of the treatment plan and resources the army is providing him. So pleased is Terrance's mother with his treatment plan, the family is moving to be closer to the source. Sara will miss them but she is happy that they are happy. Sara spent the remainder of her evening working on her thesis, blending her love of music with her love of words. She couldn't imagine a better marriage.

On balance it had been a wonderful day.

♦

I don't have time for this thought Sara as she grabbed her bags and headed out of the door. Sara is walking the tightrope between being a master's degree candidate and a master's degree holder. Her time is limited, split between work, school, family, and friends. It is a delicate balance but Sara is on target to complete her thesis in just a matter of months.

If left up to Sara, she would be doing school work not headed to the gas station, but today is her day to get gas. Since the "gas shortage" began, a number of tactics were being used to ration the supply. Car owners with license plates ending in an even number are allowed to get gas on certain days of the week, and owners with odd numbers got gas on another. Add to that there is a limit to how much gas car owners can purchase at a time. It is not unheard of to find after waiting for your turn in line the station had run out of gas. Needless to say, these conditions lead to creative solutions and tense times. Some car owners deal with the situation by changing license plates between cars in their households or bartering for the opportunity to buy gas. In isolated cases there had even been fist fights when tempers flared.

Listening to the radio as she drove down Ashby to San Pablo to the only local gas station that could be counted on to actually have gas, Sara heard more details on the break-in at the Democratic National Committee Headquarters at the Watergate building in Washington D.C. Sara didn't know what to think as the evidence implicating Richard M. Nixon, the sitting President continued to mount. More and more each day there were cries for his resignation or his impeachment.

Sara welcomed a break from bad news as she turned off the ignition to wait her turn in the line to buy gas. Left to her thoughts, Sara replayed the events of the past few days: Tauyna's wedding and the hours she spent happily preparing her thesis.

Amazed that the foreboding she feels for the country contrasts so sharply with the hope she feels for herself and her loved ones, but the contrast bears out one of her strongly held beliefs . . .

Two things can be true

All's well that ends

Things don't necessarily need to end well for folks to be glad when they do indeed end. At this point, the oil embargo which led to the "gas shortage" is ending, but the result is extremely expensive gas prices at the pumps. People are doing their own personal rationing, batching errands, cutting down on unnecessary driving, and in some cases, demanding more fuel efficient vehicles.

The Viet Nam war is ending; troops are being withdrawn from Viet Nam at a rapid rate. At the Oakland Army Base, the gateway into and out of Viet Nam, Sara sometimes sees their faces when they are returned to the states, which is often difficult for her. While most would agree it is a good thing the war is ending, so many returning soldiers, like Sara's neighbor, are different than when they left.

♦

Sara is on pace to complete her master's degree by end of summer, in just a few months. All of the research for her thesis is complete, her outline has been approved, and it is now just a matter of getting it done. Sara can literally see the finish line.

To the casual neighborhood observer it might seem Sara and her school friends have picked up where Taunya and her friends left off. Neighbors can often hear Sara's friends before they see them, announcing their arrival loud and clear. Meeting them at the front door, Sara always says the same thing, "Come on in, I'm not doing anything," meaning she is happy to set aside whatever she's doing.

Never a believer in all work and no play, and even though Sara's schedule is tight, she makes time for her family and friends. Every weekend, at least one of the days, usually Saturday, is spent with her children, grandchildren, and the day often includes Ben. Sunday morning is always spent at church and the rest of Sunday and free weekday hours are spent working on her thesis. But Friday and Saturday nights almost always find Sara socializing with friends.

Friday night after the swing shift ends, Sara and her coworkers travel by caravan to Esther's Orbit Room in Oakland, which is owned and managed by Little Esther–her nickname due to her small stature.

Inside, the music is loud and the crowd is boisterous. The menu is famous for its chitlins, fried chicken, oxtails, hush puppies, greens, cornbread, biscuits, sausages, and smothered Southern fried potatoes.

With Esther mingling freely with her patrons, it is a comfortable and friendly environment.

In the old days, Esther's was the place to be for everybody who wanted to have a good time, including sailors and soldiers, Black and White, just off of the ship. Many of the shipyard and railway workers, who were drawn to the area for work during World War II, helped create the Seventh Street boom which Esther benefited from in the '40s.

For many musicians, Esther's literally was home, living in a boardinghouse behind the club. Among the acts that played at Esther's through the years were BB King, T-Bone Walker, and Ike and Tina Turner. While it is no longer a live music venue, Sara and her friends enjoy the food and atmosphere. They are comfortable there.

On Saturday evenings, the fun shifts from Oakland to Berkeley. Sara and her Cal crowd frequent Giovanni's on Shattuck Avenue, one of the oldest restaurants in downtown Berkeley.

In the early '60s the original Schipani family restaurant's name was changed to Giovanni's. In 1967 business was so good a move was made a few blocks down Shattuck Avenue to a larger building. Giovanni's became known for its good food and family atmosphere where the matriarch was the primary chef who often left the kitchen to chat with the customers. Even after all these years Giovanni's continues to be a popular place to dine mainly because its fare is based on Mama Schipani's recipes, such as her Veal Scallopini and stuffed Eggplant Parmesan. Of course, Sara and her friends love the food but as important, is the unhurried service and the freedom to linger as long as they like. It's no mystery why Sara sticks to her Friday and Saturday night rituals. On both nights she is surrounded by people she enjoys in a venue where the owner makes her feel special.

Ignoring the world view, looking only at her personal landscape, with the completion of her degree in plain view, the perspective from Sara's lens is quite pleasing.

All's well that ends

\

Winter in America

"Thank you, Mr. Chairman. Today I am an inquisitor. A hyperbole would not be fictional and would not overstate the solemnness that I feel right now."

"Just listen to her voice," remarks Patrice as they sit paying rapt attention.

Patrice and Tessa are sitting with Sara in her living room and they, like so many Americans, are riveted to the televised impeachment hearings. The proceedings are like theater, the pomp and circumstance, the flowery language; *my esteemed colleague to my left, the gentlewoman from the great state of,* and the enormity of these matters hold them captive.

"It's not just the words she chooses but the way she delivers them, the cadence, and the tone. All part of the drama," adds Sara.

"My faith in the Constitution is whole; it is complete; it is total. It has limited impeachment to high crimes and misdemeanors."

"And her manner," contributes Tessa.

"Bearing, it's her bearing," corrects Sara.

"Today we are not being petty. We are trying to be big, because the task we have before us is a big one. The President has made public announcements and assertions bearing on the Watergate case, which the evidence will show he knew to be false."

"There it is!" exclaims Sara.

"Impeachable are those who misbehave, those who behave amiss or betray the public trust. A President is impeachable if he attempts to subvert the Constitution. Has the President committed offenses, and planned, and directed, and acquiesced in a course of conduct which the Constitution will not tolerate? That's the question. We know that. We know the question."

"Indeed," whispers Sara.

"We should now forthwith proceed to answer the question. It is with reason and not passion which must guide our deliberations, guide our debate, and guide our decision."

These words were spoken by the Congresswoman from Texas, Barbara Charline Jordan, a lawyer, educator, and the first Black person elected to the Texas senate after Reconstruction. These excerpts from her fifteen minute speech, Statement on the Articles of Impeachment, were given on July 25, 1974. During the Congresswoman's remarks Sara can't help but marvel at her accomplishments. Here she is today making a history-changing speech when, not even two decades ago, she was not considered for admission at her first-choice college, University of Texas at Austin, because she is Black.

"Whether you believe him, voted for him or think he's right for the job, he is the President. Growing up I can remember always being told to respect the job title irrespective of the man," says Sara lost in thought. "But in this case, it appears he has disrespected his role and the job title."

"What do you think is going to happen?" asks Tessa of no one in particular.

"I think he's done," replies Patrice emphatically.

"Well, do you think he will resign or be impeached?" asks Tessa pointedly.

"Oh, doesn't matter to me as long as he's gone," Patrice replies flippantly.

"It does matter," states Sara with finality. "If Richard Nixon resigns, he will be the first President to resign from the office, ever! It matters! His resignation would only reinforce the fallibility of man. It would mean that even someone who rose to the highest office in the land is not above frailty. Something we have always suspected, but would now know for sure."

Richard Milhous Nixon was born in 1913 in Southern California. Nixon rose through the political ranks and was elected to the office of President in November of 1969. He resigned from the Presidency in August of 1974. Congresswoman Barbara Jordan's fifteen minute speech is credited with "encouraging" imperiled President Nixon to resign from office just two weeks later, leaving the White House on the morning of August 9, 1974.

◆

Americans are battered by recent events. The country's foundation, it's façade around the world has already been cracked by the catastrophic Viet Nam war which is winding down, but the gulf is made significantly wider by the ramifications of the sitting President's resignation.

Vice President Gerald R. Ford, who had become Vice President when then Vice President Spiro Agnew resigned in disgrace, took the office of President, replacing Nixon on August 9, 1974. Without the benefit of being voted into either office, Sara did not have much confidence in President Ford. His ascension felt muddy, muddled, much like Sara's feelings about the state of the nation.

Watching the late news reports Sara is reminded by the anchorman that the economy continues to be sluggish, gas prices are problematic, and the cities infrastructures are beginning to crumble. The chasm between the well off and poor is widening, shrinking the middle and perhaps *Class* is emerging as the new *Race*. It all proves to be too much, and Sara goes to bed.

♦

Sara is always unnerved by a ringing telephone, but particularly so in the early morning, or late night. There is only one telephone in Sara's home. She has thought about getting an extension but it seemed excessive until the phone rings while she is in bed, as it is ringing now.

Miraculously, Sara makes it before the ringing stops, which speaks to the persistence of the caller and to the importance of the call. As is her practice, prior to answering, Sara prays for grace to handle the news heading her way.

"Hello," says Sara tentatively.

"Sara, it's Aunt Ora Lee. It's Tessa. She's in the hospital." Ora Lee is Sara's mother's older sister who lives several miles from Tessa in Los Angeles. The two of them are like two sides of the same coin.

Sara can't breathe, she can't think. She sits down just holding the telephone to her ear.

"Sara." She hears her name being called gently on the other end.

"What happened?" Sara asks with considerable effort.

"She is very ill. The doctor said not to tarry," replied Ora Lee, managing to be firm and gentle at the same time.

Agreeing to call back with the details, Sara promises to be at the Los Angeles airport before noon and as PSA has flights to Los Angeles every hour Sara keeps her promise.

♦

Sara had thrown her things into a small carryon bag which would allow her to bypass baggage claim. Arriving at the airport in time to purchase her ticket and comfortably make the 10:00 am flight, the gravity of the situation began to dawn on Sara. Never before had she felt the weight of being an only child. All of her life, she had basked in the glow of a spotlight that never needed to be shared. She felt utterly alone.

By the time the plane arrives at the Los Angeles airport Sara has pulled herself together and resolves to be a pillar of strength for her elderly Aunt Ora Lee and her husband, Coy. They have been instrumental in helping Sara feel comfortable with her mother's move to Los Angeles, always there making sure Tessa has all the support she needs.

Walking down the long corridor from the plane to the waiting area at the gate, Sara admonishes herself to stay strong.

Aunt Ora Lee looks tired and worried. Uncle Coy looks stoic. And Sara does her best to hold it together.

"How is she?" asked Sara as her greeting.

"She is very ill," says Ora Lee, repeating what she had shared earlier on the telephone. "She has been very ill for a while now, but chose not to tell any of us," she continues neutrally, not wanting to signal her feelings about her sister's decision to keep her illness to herself.

"How sick is she?" Sara manages again meekly, as if asking the same question over and over might yield a different answer.

"When the doctor suggested that we not tarry, he meant it. We need to go to the hospital directly," replies Ora Lee.

♦

Although traffic is light, Sara keeps checking her watch for the time. She is wearing her only watch, the one with the tiny rubies and diamonds surrounding the face, the one her father had given her years ago. They arrive at the hospital, about forty miles from the airport, in less than an hour which is a record in Los Angeles traffic.

Tessa Crawford is in Intensive Care with all of the requisite tubes and medical apparatus in attendance. Upon seeing her, Sara's knees buckle but Uncle Coy is there, as usual, to catch her. Sara goes to the head of the bed and takes her mother's hand, speaking softly, letting her know that she has arrived. Tessa opens her eyes, smiles weakly and squeezes Sara's hand in acknowledgement.

As is often the case, Tessa rallied a bit for Sara's sake but at 1:15 am December 14, 1974, with Sara holding her hand, Tessa Crawford takes her last breath. Sara takes her time alerting the nurses, letting the machinery do its job. Sara sits with her mother as long as they would allow, with her aunt and uncle sitting just outside of the room.

Instead of going home with Ora Lee and Coy, Sara asks to be taken to her mother's studio apartment. They all go upstairs together and Sara made a pot of coffee.

"We are happy to stay here with you if you want us to," offers Uncle Coy.

"That would be nice," replies Sara.

They drink their coffee mostly in silence as Sara walks the interior of her mother's small space.

Of course everything is in order. Her mother's bible, just so on the small table next to the chair where her mother always sat. Directly across from the small sofa sat a small television set on a rolling stand. On each armrest of the small sofa and chair are ornate crochet doilies Sara's mother had made to protect the surfaces. In the tiny alcove serving as her closet hung Tessa Crawford's dresses, all are handmade by Tessa. Sara lightly touches each garment, marveling anew at the meticulous stitching and the uniqueness of the buttons and lace. Tears stream silently down Sara's face as she surveys her mother's home and absorbs her absence.

Sara had failed to notice this before, perhaps because each time she had visited, the small space had been filled to the rafters with their presence, but there were no knick-knacks, no bric-a-brac. Sara wonders if this was by her mother's choice or if her finances had required her to keep a close rein on spending.

Sara feels she has been a good, dutiful and loving daughter but she has regrets. Sara regrets never having visited her mother alone, spending time just the two of them. Maybe if she had, Sara might know if her mother had hated bric-a-brac.

Sara regrets not knowing how her mother spent her evenings. Did she listen to the radio, watch television, read her bible? Was she lonely or content in her solitude?

Sara regrets talking about herself so much; talking about her children, her job, her degrees, always sharing what she was doing and not asking more questions about her mother's life. It seems a shame that we always become intensely interested in people only after they are gone.

No doubt Sara feels the magnitude of her mother's passing, but it feels bigger than that. On closer inspection, it feels like the passing of an era, the passing of a certain "kind of woman." It feels like the passing of the kind of woman who put the good of the family before her own good. It feels like the passing of the kind of woman who never considered herself as a stand-alone entity. She was always an appendage; someone's wife, someone's mother, someone's care-giver. It never occurred to this "kind of woman" that she could have success that was hers alone. It feels like with Tessa Crawford's passing, women of a certain "kind" were laid to rest.

It feels like winter in America

♦

Sara may have been an only child but her children willingly took on what they could to ease the burden of planning their grandmother's burial and memorial service. Upon hearing the news, Patrice and Tessa flew down to help close their grandmother's studio apartment. That task done, and the burial details taken care of, Uncle Coy drove the small group including Aunt Ora Lee back to Berkeley.

The seven-hour drive to Berkeley is filled with laughter and tears as they share stories of Tessa Crawford's life.

As her older sister, Ora Lee shared how she loved her sister from the minute she was born and how she had dedicated her younger years to helping Tessa "break out of her shell," constantly getting them both into trouble, and how Tessa had never seemed to mind.

Sara's daughters, Patrice and Tessa, told tales of growing up in the same house, with their grandmother providing loving care in their formative years and what joy she brought to them. She cooked delicious meals, baked wonderful breads and desserts, kept the house orderly and clean and was always there with a kind word and sound advice. She loved them hugely and they loved her right back.

Sara shared what a pleasure it has been to be Tessa Crawford's daughter, her only child. She shared the many ways in which her mother has made her feel special and valued. Telling the group how proud she is of the many wonderful traits and skills her mother had so freely shared with Sara, her family and everyone who knew her. Sara also shared that she knows she will feel her mother's love until she takes *her* last breath.

◆

Tessa and Patrice volunteer to write their grandmother's obituary because they know their mother would rather not. Before they part, after arriving back in Berkeley, Tessa suggests they meet the next morning to jot down their thoughts and have breakfast at Lois the Pie Queen, a restaurant not far from home. Patrice readily agrees.

They arrive within minutes of each other, order, and eat their meal but each falter at the finality of the task. Preparing the obituary is the worst and the best, providing an opportunity to remember while taking away the freedom to forget. How does one cram a lifetime into a few paragraphs? How does a picture say a thousand words? The process is endless and iterative. Two steps forward then a giant step backward with many meandering steps down memory lane.

At each attempt their reminiscing always followed the same script:

"She wore that pretty green satin . . ."

"What did he say when she said . . ."

"The drive to L.A., the Grapevine . . ."

"I think we should say . . ."

"Do you remember when . . ."

Before it was done, each Jameson sibling had taken a turn at committing their thoughts to paper; each faltered at the finality of the task. Ronald had ultimately completed and delivered the obituary and eulogy beautifully.

♦

Their grandmother, who loved them before she knew them, is gone. Their grandmother is gone.

It feels like winter . . .

Without her permission,
the world continued turning

People went about their business as if nothing had changed. They went to work, school, paid bills, prepared meals, all acting as if the earth hadn't come off its axis.

"Pull yourself together."

"This happens to everybody at some point."

"Life goes on."

Well meaning friends and relatives admonish Sara to *get on with it* or *get over it.* Her least favorite pep talk always includes "Life goes on." Sara spends hours wondering exactly what people mean when they say that to her, usually stated cheerfully along with a hearty slap on the back or an awkward hug. This empty phrase was never uttered by anyone who really understood Sara's relationship with her mother, because they knew that life as she knew it was not going on.

♦

Since her mother's death, Sara has prayed a lot, mostly praying for herself. She prays that the abundant gifts of love, time and attention her mother had so freely given her all of her life would be enough. She prays that those gifts would sustain her for all the years of her life and that her heart would stop hurting.

♦

Without fanfare or any announcement that it was happening, Sara's heart began to heal and hurt was replaced by a feeling of thanksgiving.

With her permission, the world continued turning

Some things got better while others got so much worse

The '70s are being called the "Me" decade, a decade where people are concerned with doing what's best for themselves without really considering the impact on others. There is a conservative backlash happening with people growing more and more tired of, in their words, "Whiny hippies, coddled poor people, and the demands of underserved minorities," creating a New Right.

Women are entering college and the workplace in higher numbers than in the recent past bringing with them issues unique to their gender and circumstances. Feminism is battling civil rights for attention and resources.

The national news is mostly unsettled and unsettling. Not all of the news is inherently bad; there are innovations in technology that are changing the very fabric of how things are done and enhancing what can be done. But in addition to the cultural changes, there are assaults on America that make it hard for Americans to catch their breath.

Just as Sara is starting to feel like herself again, she, like everyone else, is hit with one bombshell after another. There are some good things, some bad things but mostly bad things, with little or no time to recover in between.

In 1975 two attempts were made on President Ford's life in California, the first in Sacramento and the second seventeen days later in San Francisco, both in the state Sara calls home.

In 1979, at the Three Mile Island nuclear plant thousands of gallons of coolant were accidentally released into the surrounding area, bringing attention to the environment in a very disturbing way. This accident is America's most serious nuclear power plant accident in its history. The affects on human life were not immediately known.

On the heels of that one billion dollar crisis, is the Iran hostage crisis. American citizens were held captive for 444 days. After the hostages' successful release, a second energy crisis developed tripling the price of oil and sending gasoline prices over one dollar per gallon for the first time.

Also, an American Airlines Flight crashed after takeoff from O'Hare International Airport killing all 271 people aboard and two on the ground, making it the deadliest aviation incident on U.S. soil.

In an already flagging economy, Chrysler, facing bankruptcy, received government loan guarantees to help revive the company to avoid sending the country into deeper recession. On an even more hopeful note foretelling an amazing future, the '70s brought technological innovations that would change the world forever.

In the late '70s, the first personal home computer was released for retail sale, expanding personal productivity in ways never imagined by the average person.

And the way leisure time is spent was changed forever by the Atari 2600, the first successful home video game system, which popularized the use of microprocessor-based hardware and cartridges containing game code. It was the dawning of a whole new world.

♦

These days, having successfully completed her master's degree (one of her closely held secrets), Sara's focus is on plans for her retirement which is on the horizon in the not too distant future and her mood is light. Today, Sara's music can be heard through the front door, which is slightly ajar.

"Sara," called Zachary, "is it ok if I come in?" He has been asking Sara the same question since he was a little boy.

"Sure, I'm not doing anything," replies Sara, and she has been answering in the same way ever since Zachary was a little boy.

"I'm practicing this riff and I don't know if it's quite right," says Zachary putting his saxophone strap over his head. "Do you have time to listen?" Zachary asks as he puts the sax to his lips.

Knowing a response is not needed, Sara turns off her stereo and sits back listening with interest and pride. Zachary, now a student at Berkeley High, has been playing the saxophone since he joined the Jazz Band as a sixth grader at Longfellow Elementary School. Sara likes to believe he got his early interest in Jazz as a result of being a regular visitor at her home, listening to her extensive record collection and stories about the musicians.

"That's it Zachary!"Sara exclaims after several tries. "I like it."

"Thanks Sara, it's been bothering me for a while, I'm glad I came over," says Zachary sincerely.

"You and your sax are always welcome especially now that you're playing music that I can relate to," offers Sara with a smile. There was a period when Zachary was into avant-garde jazz, which is not Sara's cup of tea.

Zachary chuckles in response. Changing the subject, he shares with a smile, "I saw Carl and Rose at lunch time today. We said we'd meet up this Saturday, at your house." Of course, being that Carl and Rose are Sara's grandchildren, she has no problem with their plans.

"Good," replies Sara. "What's on the agenda for Saturday?"

"Nothing in particular, we thought we would hang out over here if that's okay with you," Zachary replies a bit sheepishly.

"Not a problem," says Sara enthusiastically. "By the way, how's Taunya and married life?"

"She's good," replies Zachary nodding his head.

Sara waits for more information but hearing none she realizes that is all she is going to get and takes Zachary's two-word answer coupled with his body language as good news. She misses Taunya, but Zachary and his music provide a different kind of light in the neighborhood. After a few more minutes of friendly chatter Zachary thanks Sara again for her help and reminds her that he will see her Saturday before he heads back next door.

Sara, looking forward to the plans for Saturday, is reminded that Zachary and her grandchildren, who are about the same age, are reaching many milestones with graduation among them. In anticipation of that day, Sara can clearly see herself back at the Greek Theatre cheering them on as they take their tentative steps into the future. It is her pleasure to support them in any way she can, including Zachary. Over the years, they have built a strong bond and it pleases Sara that Zachary, who doesn't have an extended family nearby, has meshed so nicely with hers. Not one to place too much faith in luck, Sara is grateful for the blessing of Zachary, Taunya and their mother, Vivian. Though her original friends in the neighborhood, Mary, Eva, and Leona are gone, but certainly not forgotten, their neighborhood replacements have worked out well.

Some things got better while others got so much worse

You can't drive without occasionally checking the rearview mirror

On waking, Sara begins having a running dialogue with herself, mostly about the past and how it fits into the future. It's a dialogue she has with some regularity. She tells herself the biggest problem with the past is that it doesn't stay in the past; parts of it permeate and color the future. She reminds herself, it's a packaged deal regrettably she can't pick and choose those things from the past that make her happy while dismissing the rest. And, try as she might despite her efforts, she hasn't been able to rewrite history, but is thankful she most definitely doesn't have to relive it.

Almost more than anything from her past, Sara misses the women from the old Julia Street– her mother, Mary, Mary's mother, Leona, Eva and all the rest. She misses the camaraderie and almost daily fellowship with Mary, her first friend on Julia Street. The Jameson and Grabel families moved into their new homes on the same day over forty years ago, and Mary and Sara have been friends since. They would talk for hours, solving the large and small problems of the world either in Mary or Sara's living room, or on one of their many, many walks through Berkeley. Although she understood their decision, Sara had been saddened when Mary told her they were moving.

Almost as much as the people, Sara misses the time, the era. She remembers the days when there was a sense of co-ownership of the future, particularly the futures of the children on Julia Street. She looks back fondly on the time when adults were comfortable sharing a word of praise or correction with any child in the neighborhood. She feels she no longer has an open invitation to contribute in some small way to the well-being of the children she sees passing her window every day, and that new reality troubles her.

To balance the scales, Sara is quick to acknowledge the happiness she has gotten from her newer neighbors. Sara likes Vivian, but Taunya and Zachary have been a source of happiness. Sara's living room window and their open front door have given Sara a front row seat to their growing up. Add the many times they have invited Sara into their lives and Sara has invited them into hers, she counts herself blessed.

Her own children, Tessa, Ronald, Gregory, Patrice and their children are a source of joy for Sara. Her children have always been and always will be her perfectly matched set, two sons and two daughters. Sara continues to mother them, though they are grown, and is an active and involved grandmother. While each of her children has met personal goals beyond Sara's fondest wishes, she is proud of the foundation she and Ben have provided them. Sara feels her family has been given many gifts; standing, within an extended family and a community, stability, a consistent set of people who love and care for them, a head-start, role models, an education and opportunity, and a spirit of risk-taking. Lovingly telling them from the time they were toddlers that, whenever the music plays to dance or get out.

And then there's Ben. Even now, try as she might, Sara cannot explain her relationship with Ben, even to herself.

As Sara counts down the days to retirement, she marvels at how much time she is spending in the past, but gently reminds herself . . .

You can't drive without occasionally checking the rearview mirror

Got to give it up

The day she has been waiting for has finally arrived–retirement day. Sara awakens with a sense of well being and predestination. She doesn't believe in coincidence, she believes everything happens by design. And by design, today is her birthday and today, the day she is eligible for retirement, are one and the same. It is only fitting that her birthday and retirement parties are planned for this very day. Still working on swing shift, no longer out of necessity but by choice, Sara happily agrees to a retirement luncheon at a restaurant not far from work, followed by a brief celebration at the Base for those who are unable to attend the luncheon. But the real celebration will be that night at Sara's home on Julia Street.

The luncheon and work party are full of the typical speeches full of praise for her years of service and the admonition, "Don't be a stranger," and Sara feels that most remarks are heartfelt. Over the years, Sara has enjoyed her work and her co-workers and as a result considers herself one of the fortunate ones. She knows she will always cherish her memories and be proud of the contributions she has made. Her family members looking on with obvious pride attend both work parties but duck out early to put the finishing touches on the night-time celebration.

◆

Arriving home from work for the last time at just after four in the afternoon on November 12, 1982, Sara pulls into her driveway and can hear music playing and people talking, having a good time inside. Rather than rushing inside Sara turns off the ignition, puts the key in her handbag and just sits. She finds she needs some separation between before and after, time between then and now, breathing space between being employed and retired. Sara has been working for over forty years with little time off, with the exception of yearly vacations and the birth of her four children. Every job she has ever held has been with the United States Government– the Richmond Shipyards, the downtown Berkeley Post Office, and Military Ocean Terminal Bay Area at the Army Base. Sara believes tomorrow, for the first time in over forty years, she will be completely unemployed and is delighted by the thought. She grabs her handbag and shawl and heads inside to join her party.

It was nearly idyllic

"Baseball, are you sure she said baseball?" asks Tessa incredulously as she and Carl walk up the steps to Sara's house. The question is answered by the roar of the crowd coming from the television as they cross the threshold into the living room. To their right, on the sofa is Sara engrossed in a televised baseball game just as she had promised Carl she would be.

"Mama, when did you start liking baseball?' asks Tessa not believing her eyes.

"I've always liked baseball, I just never had much of a chance to watch until I retired," replies Sara enthusiastically.

"But you never mentioned liking it before," continues Tessa as though she was discovering something about her mother that changes everything.

"I image there are a lot of things I haven't mentioned," says Sara clearly enjoying creating a bit of a mystery.

"But baseball." says Tessa, letting the thought die.

"What else you got going on Grandma?" asks Carl playfully, knowing he could say just about anything to his grandmother and she would be delighted by it, and by him. "Anything else you've been hiding?"

Playing along with the joke, Sara shares, "If you must know, I have watched a few basketball games since I've been home, but baseball is my favorite. I like the Giants and the A's but I like specific players from other teams. I enjoy the elegance of the plays and the pace of the game, it's lyrical. It intrigues me; there is so much more going on than meets the eye. Kind of like with me," adds Sara, clearly directing this comment at Tessa.

"I don't think I've heard you so excited about anything, other than a song or a phrase, unless it's your grandchildren," replies Tessa enjoying the moment.

"I know, it surprises me, too," shares Sara. "Between watching baseball live and recording games on my new VCR, I'm having the time of my life."

Sara is taking her folklorist role seriously. In addition to taping baseball, she tapes documentaries, live performances and TV shows, and then invites the family over for viewing and commentary.

"Who's your favorite, Grandma," asks Carl, enjoying the light banter. He is pleased to see that Sara is taking to retirement so easily, he had been afraid she would miss work. Now, looking at her it is clear she doesn't.

"It's gotta be Daryl Strawberry! He's a rookie playing for the Mets. He's six foot six and just his physical presence is intimidating in the batter's box. It's the fact he can hit a home run at anytime. That can really intimidate his opponents. I know he has had problems off the field and I would not want you to emulate him, but he is an exciting baseball player," replies Sara settling into the topic. "Of course, closer to home, playing for the A's is Rickey Henderson."

Listening to the continuing exchange between her mother and son, Tessa accepts that maybe there are things she doesn't know about her mother, acknowledging like most people, Sara must have secrets she keeps to herself; accepting that maybe it isn't a bad thing.

The rest of the day unfolds slowly and comfortably as other family members, including Ben, arrive at the house on Julia Street. Each new arrival incredulously comments on the baseball game, each wondering silently how long baseball on TV will take the place of music on the stereo.

♦

Since retiring, Sara spends her time doing whatever catches her fancy. Her days start out the same, whether a week day or a weekend. She gets up at about 7:00 am, takes her time getting dressed, turns on the television to watch the morning news and makes a pot of coffee before walking down to the corner store to buy a newspaper. She knows there is always the option of having the paper delivered but she chooses to go get it, getting out in the fresh air and sunshine. Every day of retirement offers fresh air and sunshine. Back home, Sara has breakfast and her first cigarette of the day along with a cup of coffee while doing the crossword puzzle, in ink. And so marks the end of Sara's daily routine, most days after she sets the paper aside she just follows her heart.

It was nearly idyllic

It doesn't seem like yesterday,
it seems like everyday

"Hi there," he says.

"Hello," she responds.

This seemingly uneventful exchange had gone on everyday for almost a week at a little record shop on the Southside of Chicago called Billie's or to those in the know, Lady Day's. She has noticed him noticing her, but didn't pay it much attention. He seems older, not by much, and he is handsome, really handsome. He is tall like her and angular where she is all soft curves. *Maybe it's nothing*, she tells herself.

Sara, a creature of habit has stopped in the shop on her way from work, everyday. Like clockwork, within minutes of her arrival, there he is, all six-foot-something of him, quietly flipping through a stack of LPs without ever taking his eyes off of her. Maybe she should have guessed right then that he had no real interest in music, but it had never dawned on her that he would be in a record shop every day, just to see her.

At last, on the seventh day of their dance, he approaches her and asks about the stack of records she is flipping through. She sees him moving toward her out of the corner of her eye and braces herself for the nearness of him.

"Nothing really," she replies to his question. "I like to stop in to see if they have anything new."

"Did you find anything?" he asks.

"Maybe," she answers.

He takes one step closer. "I'm Ben," he shares just above a whisper.

"I'm Sara," she replies extending her hand.

There they had stood, looking for a reason to linger, when finally Sara takes a small step in the direction of the door. In response to her movement Ben says "See you tomorrow."

And he does. And the day after, and the next day, and the next day until at last, he asked her on a date. Sara accepts his invitation suggesting he join her and some friends at a neighborhood spot Friday night. He agrees to meet her at 9:00 pm.

Sara dresses for the night in one of her favorite outfits, a fitted wool suit in shades of sable, with dark sable colored velvet lapels. Her accessories included small golden earrings, a golden wristwatch and a beautiful face framing evening hat. She is pleased with her reflection in the mirror when she finishes dressing.

Although it was crowded with people wall to wall Sara sees him as he walks through the door at exactly

9:00 pm. Although she and her friends are seated half way down the length of the crowded bar, he looks right at her. Although he needs to pay attention to his footing as he navigates the crowd, he looks only at her. She has never forgotten that look.

It doesn't seem like yesterday, it seems like every day

♦

Sara feels a bit restless and decides to get an early start on her errands. It is not quite 9:00 am, but she is not interested in the crossword puzzle or the news. Just as she had secured her seatbelt she is startled by knocking on the driver's side window, jerking to see who was there, she recognizes a man from the neighborhood, from Ben's days on Sacramento Street.

Sara tries to steady her pulse as she rolls down the window.

"Good morning," she offers neutrally.

"Good morning, Miss Ben," he replies using a name she's been called by Ben's acquaintances for years.

"How are you?" she asks warming up a bit.

"I'm fine ma'am, but it's Ben, he's asking for you," replies the man from the neighborhood whose name has not been offered nor does Sara recall it.

Sara feels herself tense up as she asks somewhat bewildered, "Asking for me, what do you mean, he's asking for me?"

Sara hears almost nothing of his response except ambulance, Kaiser in Oakland, envisioning the last time she had been summoned to the hospital on Ben's behalf and all of the accompanying issues. "What's happened," she snaps somewhat rudely.

Having been in attendance that night all those years ago, the still unnamed man was quick to reply, "No ma'am, it's nothing like that, he's sick, ma'am."

Crumbling behind the steering wheel Sara asks gently, "Will you ride with me?"

Equally gently, he replies, "Yes ma'am, I will."

They ride in silence which seems to suit both of them. Sara drives down Sacramento Street for as long as she can before getting to Mac Arthur Blvd. She avoids the freeway, not trusting her reflexes.

Sara hasn't been in a hospital since her mother died ten years ago. By most timetables ten years is a long time, but not long enough to recover from one heart-break and perhaps brace for another.

At the information desk, Sara is of no use but Jim, she heard him give his name as Jim, fills the gap. They find the way to the nurse's station on Ben's floor and again Jim explained their situation.

Assuming facts not in evidence, the nurse says to Sara, "As you might imagine, at this point all we are able to do is try to keep him comfortable."

Mistaking Sara's stunned silence as an invitation to continue, the nurse adds "He is on quite a bit of pain medication, most of which makes him sleep, so you will not get much out of him in the way of conversation, but just sitting with him will bring him comfort."

"What are you saying, I don't know what you're saying to me," shares Sara through tears.

Recognizing her mistake the nurse asks, "How much do you know about your husband's condition?"

Jim steps in asking firmly, "Maybe Mrs. Jameson could have a seat and a cup of water while you clarify what's going on." Taking his suggestion they convene in a small private waiting room as Sara's life changes again–forever.

♦

Two weeks seems like a long time but not nearly long enough when there are almost fifty years to review, which is how Sara spends most of her time while sitting at Ben's bedside. The nurse had been correct, the pain medication causes him to sleep most of the time and when he is awake he is rarely lucid.

So that she is able to remember everything or as much as possible, Sara tries her best to "batch" her memories. First, she tries to group them by year, starting at the beginning, then she tries to integrate people of significance into the year they became a part of the memory. She finds it comforting to add a framework to her grief.

◆

Sara recalls the first time she brought Ben home. Her father had been less than enthusiastic and her mother had been kind, but her mother was always kind, so that was no indication of how she really felt. Over time, they had all grown fond of one another, until they weren't. But that no longer mattered. And Sara promised herself she would not view her memories through tainted lenses.

◆

Sara remembers the family's first weeks in Berkeley living in Mrs. Knight's boardinghouse while the finishing touches were being made on their new home on Julia Street. She thinks fondly of how Ben had moved to Berkeley, found a job and a place for them to live, and prepared a new life for their family, all of which had changed their lives. Of course she couldn't think of the boardinghouse without thinking of her first friend in Berkeley, Leona. Ben had genuinely liked Leona and was saddened at her premature death.

◆

Sara thinks of their years on Julia Street and the quiet moments she and Ben had spent in companionable silence with him reading the newspaper as Sara read a book. Sara could envision their daughter, Tessa sitting at Ben's feet, content as he silently stroked her hair. Or the times, after a long day at work when he would go upstairs to their master bedroom to take a nap before dinner, and Patrice would find him sleeping with a burned-out cigarette between his lips. Patrice would wordlessly remove the cigarette as he opened his eyes, only long enough to smile at her.

◆

Although Sara is not viewing the past through tainted lenses nor is she wearing rose colored glasses, realizing that one of the problems with the past is all of it happened. It can't be rewritten, glossed over or erased, confirming that a love story isn't always lovely. Sara can't dismiss the women from the past, the heartbreak that went along with them. Sara can't dismiss the way she felt about herself as a result of the women and everything that went along with them. They cannot be overlooked or revised. It happened, all of it. Sara can't change the past but she doesn't have to dwell on the parts that broke her heart. Instead, Sara focuses on anything that doesn't bring sadness, like Ben and Carl, the countless hours they had spent together at the house on Julia Street and the many trips they had taken to see Ben's handiwork around Berkeley–just as he had done when the Jameson siblings were young.

♦

Ben left this life on a sunny afternoon in June. For the first time, Sara wishes she had paid closer attention to the many homes and businesses Ben had worked on so she could share the details with others. It seems a shame to become intensely interested in people only after they are gone.

♦

Maybe she had wished to join a tribe, a clan, a club, a rowdy, boisterous fellowship; all for one, one for all. Maybe he had longed for one-on-one, he and she against the world; intimacy, closeness, familiarity, but neither one had informed the other.

May the best woman win

This is new, thinks Sara, *there's actually a name for it.* Sara muses further, considering when her dear friend Leona died, her status didn't change. When her beloved mother died, everything changed, but Sara's status remained the same. But with Ben's passing, Sara instantly became a widow.

Eager to find meaning and context for her new status, Sara finds the definition of widow in the dictionary; a woman who has lost her husband to death. Seeking further enlightenment, she turns to her Bible. The Biblical definition feels more accurate, it speaks to the cultural changes a woman who is widowed goes through; she is set aside from the group. The Bible explains the change in her status in the eyes of others and the assumptions that are made as a result. What isn't explained is the seemingly open invitation to share those assumptions.

As a result of Sara's new status, people are quick to shroud Sara in widow's grief or strip her of the right to grieve at all, based entirely on their assumptions. Sara's relationship with Ben proves to be as complicated in death as it was while he was living.

♦

Sometimes there is no why.

"Why are you making the arrangements, I thought you were separated?"

"Why are you closing up his home, you've been apart for so long?"

"Why has this hit you so hard, I thought you were done?"

Sometimes there is no why.

♦

Questions are plentiful.

"After all these years, what is he to you?"

"What does his death have to do with you?"

"Isn't there someone else to deal with this?"

"How long is this going to affect you?"

All good questions. If she chooses, Sara needs only answer them for herself.

◆

Sara finds grief a formidable opponent with a wide arm span, knocking her down when she least expects it.

She finds grief insidious, causing harm in a gradual way.

She finds grief seeping into everything, that sadness summons sadness.

She's reminded grief is not something one gets over. There is no flip side to grief, no pushing through it. There is only acceptance of grief, absorbing grief, making adjustments as a result of grief, and finally understanding that you are altered because of grief. Sara had read these words when Leona died and they had stuck, made sense, resonated, had echoed her own thoughts each time she experienced grief.

◆

Sara also finds that grief comes bearing gifts.

Grief brings the gift of solitude, suggesting most important work in life requires being alone.

Grief brings the gift of recollection, pointing out that going forward requires, occasionally, looking back.

Grief brings the gift of bargaining, negotiating with God, leading to personal changes and growth.

Because Sara graciously accepts all gifts, she absorbs her grief in solitude, accepts her grief through recollection, and is altered by her grief through conversations with God.

The best version of the woman won

After it all

.

After it all

She don't dismiss nothing.

Sara is more mindful of the power of her thoughts.

Sara is more careful of what she says out loud.

Sara thinks twice.

Sara acknowledges there is good *and* evil in the world.

Sara actively partners with God.

After it all

Sara is not superstitious, but is respectful of all superstitions, not wanting to tempt fate:

Don't put your purse on the floor; you will never have any money.

Don't sweep your feet; you will never get married.

Don't put a hat on the bed; someone will die.

Don't step on a crack, open an umbrella indoors, walk under a ladder or split a pole.

Sara knows them all. This ain't the half of it.

After it all

Since her family and friends have moved out of the neighborhood there are few pop-in visitors. Sara misses the drop-ins.

Since Sara finished school and Zachary's family moved away, it's rare now that Sara hears her name being called from the open front door. The front door is rarely left open.

Without Ben, there is no more "two taps" on the front door before someone comes inside. Sara finds herself listening for Ben's taps.

After it all

In a complete about face, Sara prefers the longer days of summer over the darker days of winter.

On balance, Sara is at peace, knowing there are more days behind than in front of her.

Because hers is the opinion that matters most and her internal clock is the only clock she heeds, she knows instinctively when she is ready.

After it all

Free from the overwhelming sadness of death, Sara speaks freely of those that have passed on. She is able to share a funny story, tell a tall tale, or say the things they used to say. Never one to use bad words, feeling at first she was too young, feeling now that she is too old, Sara has suspended her no bad words rule, choosing to quote Ben, often. "In the words of Ben," she says before letting hell or damn fly freely. Now, liberally sprinkled in Sara's conversations are comments like, "Just like Mama would say," or "If Mama was here she'd say…" It's so common that her family and friends regularly have a laugh at her expense. Sara's favorite is when Gregory Brown, her son Gregory's best friend, quips, "Your grandmother is the chattiest dead woman I know." Sara can laugh with the rest of them.

She don't dismiss nothing.
She dismisses everything.

Making America great again

Sara is putting herself back together again and creating a new norm. Though they no longer live within walking distance, her family, children and grandchildren, are regulars in her home, again. Music and laughter are regulars in her home again. Weekends, Saturdays or Sundays after church find some combination of family and friends visiting companionably.

On one such afternoon, Sara is drawn into a conversation between two of her older grandchildren. "Can you believe people actually fell for 'Let's make America great again' and what about 'It's morning again in America!'" exclaims Carl referring to the campaign slogans Ronald Reagan used in his bids for the presidency in 1980 and now, in 1984.

"Well, he is an actor," replies Rose.

Sara listens with some discomfort as her grandchildren discuss the president and the state of the nation. She has always believed it is proper to respect the job if not the man, and she is uncomfortable with the tone of their conversation. She bites her tongue as long as she can before offering her thoughts. She knows she will have to say something if not in defense of the man, out of respect for the office.

In spite of the importance of the recent presidential election, Sara has not been engaged. She has been involved in her own personal concerns, during the 1980 election season she was happily preoccupied with her upcoming retirement and feeling a general sense of well being, she had paid minimal attention. During the recent election, she was overwhelmed by Ben's death she had cared even less. Both times Sara had not been particularly attentive to the running of the country. But now, hearing Carl and Rose's comments, she is reminded of the rights and responsibilities they all carry.

♦

Giving it further thought, Sara reminds herself that things resonate with people if they directly impact them, could happen or have happened to them, or a loved one. She smiles as she thinks of President Truman's old saying, *"It's a recession if your neighbor is out of a job but it's a depression if you are."*

During the years leading up to the 1980 presidential election Sara had been mostly satisfied with the state of the nation and her place in it. She had been impressed with the decency President Carter displayed while in office and, with the exception of the Iran Hostage situation, was comfortable with the thought of him serving another term. For the most part life had been good for Sara and those in her circle, so from her perspective the country was not experiencing a recession, depression or any conditions that required severe change or alteration.

But in the recent past, there had been events, close to home, that had shaken Sara to her core and were impossible to forget, like the Chowchilla kidnapping in July of 1976. One bright summer day twenty-six elementary school children and their bus driver on the way back to school from a field trip were kidnapped by armed gunmen. The kidnappers had imprisoned the victims inside a buried moving -van with only a small amount of food and water. Thankfully, after a number of hours, the bus driver had been able to escape, freeing the group. The children did not come from wealthy families; they were just children whose parents loved them, just like Sara's own grandchildren. The randomness and the plausibility of that kind of incident happening again terrified Sara and most every parent who was aware of the story. Sara's thoughts are scattered, more emotional than chronological, taking her in no particular order from one horrific event in recent history to another.

She recalled, in November of 1978, after following cult leader, Jim Jones, from San Francisco to Guyana in South America, over 900 followers committed suicide in mass at his behest, following his example. Sara knows there is evil in the world and credits this act to pure evil. She does not hold the country's leaders accountable for this tragedy, she knows they have no weapons against evil. That reality terrifies Sara.

♦

Americans clearly wanted change. In the 1980 election the Republican candidate Ronald Reagan handily defeated President Carter with what many in the opposing party referred to as *style over substance*. Many believed that his acting talent and training paid off, landing Reagan in the White House. It was during that successful bid for election that Mr. Reagan began using the slogan, "Let's make America great again," referring to shoring up the sagging economy, and lowering the high unemployment and inflation rates.

At the same time, as President-elect Reagan's luck would have it, or more accurately, as a result of complex negotiations by the Carter administration, the Americans who had been held hostage in Iran for 444 days, despite a failed rescue attempt under President Carter's administration, were released on the very day President Reagan took office, January 20, 1981, affirming to those who voted for him that they had made the right choice. The hostage release, the high point in President Reagan's presidency, would not be matched again during the eight years he was in office. Almost immediately after the hostages were released, President Reagan's popularity began to wane.

♦

Although her children and grandchildren are adults, Sara never stops being concerned for their well being. Add to that, two of her four children, her matched set, are broken. The issues they face are beyond Sara's capabilities, but not her prayers. These days Sara is leaning heavily on her partnership with God.

Is America great, again?

Rising tides don't lift all boats

Relying on his skill as a master communicator and capitalizing on the good will he built with his optimistic can-do approach, President Reagan was credited with reversing the pendulum swing from despair to confidence, decline to renewal, earning a second term in office in 1984, defeating Democratic rival Walter Mondale by a landslide. The new campaign slogan, "It's morning again in America" was a simple message, which along with President Reagan's delivery resonated with Americans.

At the same time there is a pervasive cultural change in the country. Americans are embracing glitz and Hollywood Glamour, exemplified by President and Mrs. Reagan. Fear fueled the '80s, fear of failure, of poverty, of living below other people's expectations. Underscoring the mood, during this era, so many new millionaires were created that the word "millionaire" lost its significance. *New money* became *Old money*. Money is being spent faster than it can be made. Silicon Valley and Wall Street have taken on new meaning to some but have little meaning to the average person.

In contrast to all the conspicuous consumption, homelessness, the AIDs epidemic, crack addiction and the plight of the mentally ill who have been left adrift due to recent closures of mental hospitals plague the inner cities and city centers. Instead of the fruits promised by "trickle-down economics," an ever widening gulf separates the rich and poor, as greed, fear, and loathing seep into the cultural norm. Rather than "Morning in America," for some it is the darkest of nights.

By the mid '80s the economy is on the mend, referred to by some as another Gilded Age, The Roaring 80s. But a paper economy is dismantling the manufacturing plants across the country, including Berkeley. Blue collar jobs are being replaced by white collar careers. The number of disenfranchised grows while the middle class shrinks. Property values increase, pleasing homeowners, but rents are raised exorbitantly, forcing hard working families into homelessness.

Rising tides don't lift all boats

Morning again in America

"It doesn't matter who the President is," says Carl flatly.

"Yeah, I don't think it much matters," replies Rose, with resignation.

"I mean really, does what they do in Washington D.C. really affect us all that much here in Berkeley?" asks Carl.

Before joining the conversation on a leisurely Sunday afternoon in her living room, Sara wanting to make her words count, searches for examples that might resonate with her grandchildren. As human nature dictates, she thinks first of the most deeply felt events of the recent past and their impact on the country.

One by one in rapid succession Sara's thoughts take her back to that afternoon in July of 1984 when life for Americans took a turn in a most cruel and unfathomable way. Families, mothers, fathers, children, friends were out having a meal, eating a snack, enjoying each other before heading home, to a soccer practice, or to a friend's house when the unimaginable happened. A man

126

with a gun opened fire on people he had likely never met, or had likely never even seen before, killing twenty-one and injuring nineteen. The randomness and the possibility of it, or something equally horrific happening again, left Sara and the country, perhaps the world, unnerved and unsteady and unspeakably sad.

Because fear opens the door for fear, Sara thinks about the morning that had started just like all the other mornings, with a walk to the corner store to get the newspaper, and then back home for a cup of coffee, the crossword puzzle, and the morning news on TV. Sara had been engrossed in her puzzle when she heard the newscaster say, "Something's wrong." Those two words captured Sara's attention. The next two words, "My God," broke her heart. Right before her eyes, and those of everyone watching, the Challenger Space Shuttle had exploded, instantly killing the astronauts on board. The civilian teacher, the racially diverse crew, all killed instantly. The randomness, the possibility of something equally horrific happening again and the fact there is no safeguard against it left Sara and the country and perhaps the world, unnerved, unsteady and unspeakably sad.

Corralling her thoughts before they got completely away from her, understanding these events were beyond the country's leaders' control, Sara tries to think of events that are more closely tied to the country's leaders' choices to help make her point to her grandchildren.

Asking the question of no one in particular, "What about the situation in downtown Berkeley or even right next door?" she asks cryptically.

"What do you mean, Grandma?" asks Rose, genuinely confused.

"On more than one occasion I've listened to each of you voice your displeasure with the changes that are happening downtown. And I've heard you when you've wished for a solution to the problem happening next door," replies Sara.

◆

Prior to the 1970s, Berkeley residents saw almost no homeless people sitting out on the streets in downtown Berkeley. Shops and businesses on Telegraph Avenue in the downtown area thrived as people shopping and conducting other business crowded the streets. Then, slowly, over the years, the city center began to change. The sight of people sleeping on the streets became increasingly common, and more and more shelters began to pop up to address the needs of the homeless population that had gone relatively unnoticed before. Berkeley, like many other cities across the nation, saw its homeless population rise as a result of changing federal policies and the economic downturn in the '80s.

In 1981, the Reagan administration deinstitutionalized the mentally ill by providing funds for state governments to create a more community-based support system of mental health departments and clinics. However, the policy ended up decreasing federal mental health spending by thirty percent. It also closed state mental health services without creating the intended community support systems, leaving many mentally ill people on the streets and adding to the homeless population.

♦

"Oh, you mean the homeless people congregated around the Bart Station downtown," Rose confirmed, acknowledging that she is starting to understand where Sara was headed. "And it's not just downtown, the problem is spreading. They have set up sort of a camp in the park across the street from Berkeley High. I am not unsympathetic, but it gets old by the time I have been asked for money by four or five different people. I know a lot of them have mental issues, but it's still tough."

"Not to mention they can get in your face if you say no," agrees Carl.

"And that situation next door, it's just sad," Rose adds. They are all aware of the situation developing next door to Sara's home as they had lived through it the first time around.

They all knew the story. Lately the young veteran Sara had helped years ago has returned to the neighborhood and resumed his walking.

According to the neighbor who lives in the house the soldier once lived in, who was told by the soldier's mother, the lack of funding means the programs that helped her son have been cut. Once again, it is not unusual for Sara to look out of her kitchen window only to find the young man sitting on the porch next door, smoking cigarette after cigarette before starting his solitary walk up and down the block. Just like old times, his mother eventually comes to take her boy back home.

"That is exactly why it matters who the President is," said Sara.

Mourning in America, again

Don't underestimate
the fullness of nothing

As the world expands through the miracle of technology, twenty-four hour news channels bringing events and faraway places near, Sara's world is shrinking by her design. In place of socializing at Giovanni's or Little Esther's, Sara spends her time in quiet contemplation at the neighborhood branch of the public library across the street from Grove Street Park, just a few blocks from home on the corners of Grove and Russell Streets.

Sara enjoys the short walk which takes her past the YMCA on the corners of Russell and California Streets, allowing her to reminisce about the many hours her children and their friends spent in pursuit of fun at the Y. They couldn't wait for Sara to get home from work to share the day's adventures in ping pong, basketball, billiards, movies or any of a number of activities. Sara had always been grateful that the activities were free and the staff was so well chosen and well-trained.

After rounding the corner onto Russell Street, to Sara's right, is the family home of one of her son

Gregory's good friends. Sara often wonders what became of them after they moved out of the neighborhood. This day is no exception. The remaining four block walk is uneventful until Sara gets to Grove Street Park, one of the regular haunts from the days when her children were old enough to walk there on their own.

"We're going to the park Mama," they would say.

"Which one?" Sara would inquire.

Depending upon what was on their agenda, the answer would be either San Pablo or Grove Street, prompting Sara to inquire further, "Who's going with you?" And so it went. There was safety in numbers.

Just seeing the façade of the Grove Street Branch of the public library lowers Sara's blood pressure and puts her in a good mood. The Asian inspired structure is seated on a well tended patch of green grass, situated back away from the busy street. Just crossing the threshold lowers Sara's blood pressure even further as she is welcomed by the softly lit open floor plan with books in all directions and as far as the eye can see.

Sara loves to read as much as she loves listening to music. If she had to pick one over the other she is not certain she could do it. As is her practice, she roams the shelves, picking up titles or authors that call to her. When she finally picks one, it is not unheard of for her to read until closing, or until she has finished with her selection, whichever comes first. Only when she hasn't finished with her selection does she check out her book to finish it at home. Sometimes, when the day has gotten away from her, Sara finds herself walking the short distance home in the dark. That habit has recently been broken as the blocks between the library and Sara's home are no longer within her comfort zone. Where there were once single-family homes filled with people Sara knew or at least recognized, there are now large apartment buildings filled with people Sara rarely saw—not unlike the landscape on Sara's block.

♦

At this point on Julia Street, the neighbors to Sara's right are a young Hispanic family, mother, father and two small children. Sara knows them only to wave hello and by the cultural music they play. To Sara's left are UC Berkeley students, all three White males. Sara assumes they are pretty serious students because she doesn't hear a peep out of them and sees them only in passing. The other residents on the street are equally diverse.

The police bus which was parked on the corner of Sacramento and Julia Streets is gone as is the visibly suspicious activity that brought it there. The makeup of the businesses on Sacramento Street has changed. The cleaners, shoe repair, doctors' office, beauty shop and post office are all gone. Gone are the liquor store, tiny night club, and pool hall which were all in a row and now replaced by a large laundry mat. Also gone are the young men who had stood in front. Sara often wonders what has become of them, hoping against hope that it is something good. Mirroring the neighborhood, the hustle and bustle has gone out of Sara's daily round as well. Where Sara's days were once filled to the brim with activity, at this point in her life she is comfortable looking at an expanse of empty hours.

She appreciates the fullness of nothing

Again

Free time gives Sara the freedom to think, muse, ponder and plan. Since her retirement, she has the option to fill her time with something – or nothing at all. She considers it the reward for a job well done, or at least a job that *is* done.

En route to her monthly lunch with former coworkers who are also old friends, Sara finds herself sitting at the stop light on Broadway in downtown Oakland, before making her way into Jack London Square. Just in view is a small group of women who appear to be on their lunch hour, crossing with the light in front of her. For no particular reason, and not particularly a reflection of the outfits they're wearing, Sara is reminded of the cyclical nature of life reflected with surprising regularity in fashion– what goes around comes around. Musing further, she remembers the well worn fashion axiom, "If you are old enough to have worn it the first and/or second time it was fashionable, please don't wear it the third time around." Sara chuckles.

As the light holds, Sara has time to extend her thoughts. Thinking of the issue she tried to resolve via telephone earlier in the day, she decides the same difficult situation and the same type of difficult people should only have to be dealt with once in a lifetime. She chuckles as the light turns green. Sara admits, if only to herself, she can be somewhat inflexible when it comes to difficult people. Acknowledging, once she's done, she stays done.

As she makes her way into the covered parking structure closest to Kincaid's, Sara considers herself fortunate to have her steadfast group of lunch buddies. They are among her favorite people who have been hand selected over the years, who fit nicely together and always have a great time. Parking the car Sara is confident that today won't be an exception.

Always nostalgic after lunch with old friends, having spent most of their time talking about old times, Sara chooses to drive back home through the neighborhood where she and her family spent their first weeks in Berkeley before moving into their home on Julia Street. The old boarding house, near Alcatraz and Harmon, is still there, but is no longer a boarding house. Mrs. Knight has long since gone to her reward.

As Sara drives through neighborhoods which were once well tended and populated with homes owned primarily by Colored people– as Black people were called in the early '40s, Sara's thoughts turn more serious. In her lifetime, she has been called Colored, Negro, Black, African American, and other names she chooses to ignore but Black is her favorite. Maybe James Brown is to blame. Along with other people's labels, came their consequences, their attitudes, and their expectations.

Appreciating the beauty of free time, Sara takes the leisurely route home allowing her thoughts to take her wherever they want to go. As she drives north on Grove Street her thoughts circle back to the cyclical nature of life without any judgment, not deciding if it's a good or a bad thing, but that it is a reality. Sara notes that in some ways she feels she is caught in a loop, almost like a reel-to-reel tape, or a long-playing album. Maybe everyone's album is different, but it's full of songs that are familiar and reminiscent of one another. Some of Sara's songs are mournful, some joyful, some despairing, but most are hopeful. The down side of her loop, her album, feels like she is reliving certain segments, as if she has seen them before, like history repeating itself, as if the lessons haven't been learned. But on the upside, the loop combines sweet songs with treasured memories.

♦

During their first days in Berkeley, in the 1940s and early1950s, Sara participated in the "Don't buy where you can't work," national effort to have Colored people be accepted as employees at businesses where they were grudgingly accepted only as customers. It was a somewhat successful nation-wide, non-violent boycott of businesses which resulted in more jobs for Colored workers. However, major job gains were not realized until the 1964 Civil Rights Act was passed. A problem with unlocking memories is they all come rushing back at once, and if you're not careful, the bad ones push their way to the front of the line.

Sara reviews the loop of unrest and rioting she has seen more than once in her lifetime. Most vivid in review are the riots in the 1960s in Watts, in predominantly Black neighborhoods. The genesis that time, two White policemen had pulled over a Black motorist suspected of drunk driving. A crowd had gathered near the corner of Avalon Boulevard and 116th Street as the arrest unfolded, the spectators growing angry by what they believed to be yet another incident of racially motivated abuse by the police. Fueled, some say, by years of economic and political isolation, some of the residents of Watts rebelled and began to riot in protest. The rioters eventually ranged over a 50-square-mile area of South Central Los Angeles, looting stores and torching buildings as snipers fired at random targets. When thousands of National Guardsmen intervened, the rioting ceased. After five days 34 were dead, 1,032 injured, nearly 4,000 arrested, and $40 million worth of property was destroyed. The Watts riot was the worst urban riot in twenty years and fore-shadowed the many rebellions to occur in ensuing years in Detroit, Newark, and other American cities. Another case of history repeating itself, perhaps lessons had not been learned.

Again in1992, again in Los Angeles, four White Los Angeles police officers were caught on video while beating an unarmed Rodney King, an African-American man. The officers were indicted, tried and all were acquitted of any wrongdoing in the arrest, despite what some felt was damning evidence caught on an eighty-six second video clip.

Hours after the verdicts were announced, outrage and protest turned to violence. After five days 55 were dead, almost 2,000 were injured, 7,000 were arrested, with nearly $1 billion in property damage. Sara felt she had seen it all too many times before.

In late June of 1994, just weeks after Rodney King was awarded almost $4 million in a civil suit, across town OJ Simpson was charged with the murder of his estranged wife and a male friend. Sara, like everyone else, watched the bizarre circumstances surrounding the arrest, and like everyone else, instinctively braced for the aftermath.

Deliberately pushing back these thoughts as well as those that tried to sneak in with them, Sara beckoned best loved memories to the fore. Like an enthralled bystander she lets the loop encircle her. There are sweet spots in the loop.

Sara is sweetly reminded of all the *Firsts*.

First words, first steps, first days of school, first blush, first light, first relationships and first heartbreaks.

She remembers the *New Starts*.

New jobs, new homes, new ideas, births and deaths.

And of course, *The Lasts*.

Last days, last laughs, last songs, last dances, last chances, last words, and last looks.

Ever- lasting.

And with them, she embraces all the people, all the places and all the moments.

And she would happily relive them all again.

And Again

Just a couple of forevers

1974, 1984 and again in 1994, sadness fell on the fours. Sara's mother, Tessa Crawford, died in December of 1974, Ben Jameson died in July of 1984, and Sara Jameson died in August of 1994, just shy of her 74th birthday. By all standards, ten years is a long time, but not nearly long enough to recover from one blow and brace for the next.

Since the first time, the pattern had never varied; one would call the other to meet at Lois the Pie Queen, a neighborhood spot, first thing for breakfast. They would eat, talk about kids, jobs, current events, anything to slow down the meal. On the way out, they'd linger as they paid the bill, visit with the cashier, reading the postings on the wall highlighting neighborhood news before heading to the parking lot. Once situated behind the wheel, they drove slowly, single file, going even slower the closer they got to their destination.

Arriving within minutes of each other they park their cars, gather their supplies and take the short walk up the short walkway, and up the three steps. With Tessa at her side, Patrice reaches for the knob but their memories always stop them at the door of the house on Julia Street.

Backing away from the threshold Patrice sighs, saying, "I can't do this today."

"It's okay, we don't have to," reassures Tessa, "let's go have lunch."

In response, Patrice smiles weakly, "We just had breakfast."

"I know," Tessa invariably replies, "but what we need is lunch."

♦

Preparing the obituary had been the worst and the best, providing an opportunity to remember, but at the same time, taking away the freedom to forget. How does one cram a lifetime into a few paragraphs? How does a picture say a thousand words? The process had been endless and iterative. Two steps forward then a giant step backward with many meandering steps down memory lane. Their reminiscing always followed the same script.

"She wore that pretty green satin…"

"What did he say when she said…"

"The drive to L.A., the Grapevine…"

"I think we should say…"

"Do you remember when…"

♦

Each Jameson sibling had taken a turn at committing their thoughts to paper; each faltered at the finality of the task. Each Jameson sibling asked the questions, "How does one cram a lifetime into a few paragraphs, how can a picture say a thousand words?" Each Jameson sibling knew to tell the story properly, they would need at least a couple of forevers.

♦

This time Tessa Jameson, the oldest of the Jameson children, with a new resolve, was ready for the task at hand. This time they had to push through. There was work to be done, no time for reminiscing. The new tenants were moving into the house on Julia Street, the home the Jamesons had moved into in 1943, all those years ago.

In spite of her resolve, Tessa allowed herself a brief daydream, remembering move-in day clearly.

Their belongings had been packed in the bed of a borrowed pick-up truck with the family seated in front. She fondly remembers her younger brother, Ronald, asking the questions she also wanted answered as they drove to the new house.

"Are there kids on our new street?" Ronald asks tentatively.

"There are lots of kids on Julia Street," Ben replies warmly.

"Is there a park?" Ronald asks with excitement.

"There are two parks within walking distance, San Pablo Park and Grove Street Park," Sara replies.

"Will they like us?" Tessa asks anxiously.

"I'm sure they will," Sara answers with her usual confidence.

Daydream over, this time it has to be different. Today they will need to push past the memories that stand guard at the house on Julia Street.

40246198R00084

Made in the USA
San Bernardino, CA
14 October 2016